THE FIREPLACE

Jason was born and bred in a village in North Bedfordshire. He has always enjoyed writing and reading across a wide range of genres. Jason works as a postman and any spare time that he has left he spends with his wife, dog, children and grandchildren.

J. Chandler

THE FIREPLACE

Olympia Publishers
London

www.olympiapublishers.com
OLYMPIA PAPERBACK EDITION

A CIP catalogue record for this title is
available from the British Library.

ISBN: 978-1-84897-664-1

(Olympia Publishers is part of Ashwell Publishing Ltd)

This is a work of fiction. Names, characters, places and incidents originate from
the writer's imagination. Any resemblance to actual persons,
living or dead, is purely coincidental.

Published in 2016

Olympia Publishers
60 Cannon Street
London
EC4N 6NP

Printed in Great Britain

To Louise, Emily and Charlotte

Prologue

She ran.

The rain pelting down around her, restricting her vision to a few steps. The branches clawed at her, dragging her to a halt, but she pulled free to stumble a few more paces before slipping and falling to the ground.

In a second she was back on her feet fighting to stem the panic she could feel rising in her breast. The hem of her cloak caught on a fallen log, snapping her head back and causing her to fall again. This time she landed hard enough to jar her teeth.

She caught herself irritably and forcibly pushed down the fears that threatened to overwhelm her.

"Think it through."

"They probably won't have even had time to organise a search party yet!" she told herself. "The dogs will be useless in this driving rain, and even though they must know where I am heading, they could make no better speed than I." With this thought in mind she resumed her passage through the wood. Everything was in her favour - for now. The rain, the darkness, the confusion, which must delay any pursuit. Although she knew well enough that the pursuit itself was inevitable.

She cursed herself for what seemed the hundredth time. If only. If only.

If only she had planned it better...

But that thought tailed off, she couldn't have reckoned on a chance discovery like that and berating herself for it would not alter the fact that she had been discovered.

She cast her mind back to earlier that evening, everything had gone so well. Befriending the girls, Gods, that had taken weeks, luring them away from their inattentive mother had been so easy. She had enticed them into a game. They were so desperate to please her, so naive, so fresh, so young. So she blindfolded them and warned them not to peek. They had both giggled and waited in anticipation for the sweet meats she had told them were hidden in the barn.

Once in the barn she led one up behind the straw bales and returning, collected the other. The two girls stood facing one another, although they could not know this. Stroking their heads and making soothing sounds she had one last look around to ensure she was on her own.

Then she got down to her art, gagging them, stripping them, binding them. Only then did she remove the blindfolds. She could see the fear in their eyes, smell it on the ether, feel it course through her veins like the most seductive yet thrilling of sensations. When she pulled the short blade from deep within her clothes and showed it to her captives she felt it rush through her again. One of them gagged and she knew it for a suppressed scream. The smaller of the two, a delicate thing with a pretty face and hair the colour of butter had wet herself.

Ah! The glory of it all.

Their fear would only make their hearts beat faster, the blood richer.

The moment of her success was so sweet she revelled in it.

The youngest girl first, let the older girl know exactly what was coming.

The knife slid between her ribs with barely any resistance and she quickly took a phial for the blood. Not that she would need this, not now. But a virgin's blood could prove useful for so many things it would almost be a crime to waste a drop of it.

Once the phial was full of the rich, red, viscous fluid she started on her butchery. It was no easy task to remove a heart in the best of circumstances, and at the back of a stable with no real light to work by presented greater difficulties.

However, she had planned for all of this. Practising with mice, small birds, even a stray sheep. She knew exactly what to do. The only problem was the thrill. She could feel herself getting excited; she began to sweat, her hands trembling.

This would not do. Not at all.

Taking a few deep breaths she quelled her feelings. Become detached. Become detached she repeated over and over. How long had she been there? Not long. Not long enough for the mother to have missed her offspring, obviously. There had been no sounds of alarm. Or had there? She couldn't say for definite in her excited state.

Would one heart be enough?

Surely it would be better to have two.

She looked for the second child; the remains of the first were covered in blood. Looking down at herself, her hands, her arms, the front of her dress. She was soaked. How had she not realised?

The second child was squirming away, almost to the door.

Quickly she became calm, she lunged after her prey and caught at a foot, drawing the body back to her.

And then the noise.

Voices.

She pulled the child back into the darker corner and thought to hide.

What was the point?

There was no way to hide what had happened.

The voices came closer, close enough for her to distinguish some of what they were saying.

They are coming in!

Why? This barn is hardly ever used except to store winter grain for the horses. It was spring.

The child, perhaps realising this was help, began to whimper behind the gag.

The voices stopped.

Had they heard? Were they coming in?

There was nothing else for it. Grabbing the girl's hair she pulled her head back and slit her throat.

She rushed to the door and risked a peek outside.

"What're you doing in my barn?"

Gods, he was right on top of her, reaching out to pull her into the open.

She stabbed quickly and caught him in the throat. He fell back and she was away.

His companion stood dumbstruck, mouth opening and closing uselessly.

She was at the edge of the wood before she heard a cry go up behind her.

"Murder!"

She brought herself back to the present.

She had one heart.

She would make sure it would be enough.

She came out from the deepest part of the wood, across the clearing to her cottage.

She opened the door and made her way to the fireplace, the only source of light. Perhaps her pursuers would be fooled by the lack of light? No, that was foolishness itself. This would be the first place they would look.

She must work. And work fast.

Taking the heart from within her cloak she placed it on the fireplace.

The carven wolves on the fire surround appeared to look at it hungrily, the glow from the embers on the grate gave the engraved beast below the mantle a demonic expression.

Everything was set for her art.

The greatest, most powerful spell she would ever cast.

Immortality.

Calling upon all her dark Gods to aid her in her task, she stood and gathered the heart to her.

Outside the driving rain was suddenly whipped by the wind so strong that it was virtually horizontal.

Clouds massed menacingly cutting off all light, except the glow from the fire.

Shards of lightning cracked around the cottage leaving great smoking holes in the earth of the clearing.

Inside she cast her arts, her Gods pleased by her blood sacrifice, lent her the powers she most needed. With the potions she had already prepared she cast the heart onto the embers of the fire.

It's energy lighting the cottage in stark relief to the dark surrounding woodlands.

Within, weird colours shone through the windows, giving the whole an otherworldly feel.

Recoiling in terror, the armed mob stood at the edge of the clearing.

None daring to set foot into the hellish scene. All looked to the Squire and the young militia captain for leadership, but both fearing for themselves were at a loss what to do. Certainly, neither was prepared to risk the clearing.

In front of the fireplace, driven to her knees, her hair flying wildly with the static energies, she pushed her hands into the flames and retrieved the heart.

Remarkably it had not heated any more than when she first stole it from the blonde girl. She ate it.

In an instant the fires died, the storm abated, the clouds dispersed. It had worked.

She could feel it.

Let them come; they could do nothing to harm her now. She stood to face the door.

After a moment's astonishment the mob surged forward. Anxious to keep a semblance of order, the Captain ordered the militia to advance.

The door crashed open and the cottage filled with men. Their original fury increased a hundredfold by their earlier fear.

None, however, would approach her.

She stood, her back to the fireplace. It was a ghastly sight. Her cloak torn, her dress covered in dried blood. Her mouth and chin still dripping fresh blood and gore from her gruesome act. Her hair still waved madly around her head.

She laughed, breaking the silence.

"You can do nothing now. Stand back, and I may let you live!"

The captain and his militia forced a path through into the room.

"By all that is Holy and the laws invested in me, I arrest you for witchcraft." The words sounded hollow in his mouth. This was not why he had joined the militia. His captaincy, bought by his father, suddenly felt heavy on his young shoulders.

He waved two men forward to seize her, but though they approached it was with such obvious trepidation that she laughed again.

"You can do nothing to harm me. Leave now!" She took a step forward and all backed up accordingly.

A young man, a relative of the murdered children, leapt forward wielding a mallet. Her hand came up and the same knife, which had ended his nieces' lives, now cut his short.

The spell broke.

The mob took charge and barged forward.

The blacksmith's hammer shot through the air, hurled with all the strength of his years at the forge, and caught her full on the forehead.

She stumbled back and fell into the fireplace. The ensuing explosion threw everyone back. Her screams chasing all as they fell from the door of the cottage. Fleeing madly, the villagers, their courage gone, ran back to the wood.

What was wrong? She could feel herself burning. It was agony, the flesh peeling from her bones. This was wrong. This should not be happening. She was immortal. Wasn't she?

One heart.

It hadn't been enough.

She screamed in terror at what she had done. Not guilt. Never that. But at the horror that it had gone wrong. One heart.

She could feel life leaving her and she strove to take it back.

Looking down she could see the remains of her body. Ash for the most part.

No pain.

No external feelings whatsoever.

Was she dead?

She didn't think so, but the alternative was too terrible to contemplate.

Not dead, but not alive.

Immortal? Yes, after a fashion. But impotent.

She could see, as if through a mist, the young captain gingerly kicking the ashes. There was nothing left of her.

One heart. It hadn't been enough.

Or had it?

Outside her pursuers had entered the clearing, a motley gathering of villagers armed with the tools of their trade. Pitchforks, mallets, the blacksmith with his hammer. All filled with fury at the sight of the small children found in the grain barn. Back by the squire and a squad of mounted militia, their bravery fuelled by revulsion, quailed at the sight of the cottage. Lightning still struck the ground in sporadic bursts, lifting the hairs on their heads.

Chapter 1

Anne Masterson guided her old Mini through the trees. Her map had said that the 'road' to the cottage was a bit rough.

"A bit rough," she said out loud, "nothing less nimble than a mountain goat could get up here."

She received a satisfying grunt from the passenger seat where Elizabeth, her eldest daughter, sat. At sixteen she was in what her psychiatrist called 'those difficult years', where a grunt spoke volumes.

The twins in the back seat laughed and then carried on with whatever game they had invented.

Following the sudden death of their father, a little over a month before, Anne had decided to take the family away from all the well-intentioned do-gooders who were, quite frankly, beginning to get on her nerves. If it wasn't cakes and pies then it was money, all given with a patronising smile. Everyone pulling together to help. What they really wanted, really needed, was time on their own to rebuild their family unit without interference. She missed him so much, and when the children were in bed and she was finally alone for the night she wept. Every night in fact since he had gone. Leaving her with a sense of loss, like when people who had had a limb removed could still feel it hurting. Although he had been away with work an awful lot he was still her right arm. Her strong right arm. The tumour that had developed so suddenly on his brain had defied the Doctor's attempts to save him and in less than a month from its discovery it had killed him, and in doing so deprived her of the only man she had ever loved.

Elizabeth, she knew, felt much the same way. Always a withdrawn girl, Dave had always brought her out of herself, given her the confidence she lacked when he wasn't there. Elizabeth needed this break as much as she did. She looked over at her eldest child and smiled. Of her three children Elizabeth most resembled her. The same brown hair although Elizabeth's was long whereas hers nowadays only just touched her shoulders in a rather boring but serviceable bob. And whereas Anne still liked to think she hadn't lost her good looks, matured like a fine wine Dave had always joked, Elizabeth leaned more towards attractive than pretty.

In her rear-view mirror the twins, Victoria and Mary, were still absorbed with each other. Which was how it had always been. Pretty little girls, both small, skinny, blonde. At times she had wanted to tattoo the pair of them with their initials to tell them apart better. Lovable rogues was how Dave had always described them, innocently mischievous. Completely dependant on one another, to the exclusion of everyone else. At nine years old there was a seven-year age gap between them and their elder sister. A result of over doing the wine one-year at Dave's works Christmas do. But she loved them all the same.

Of all of them the twins had coped best with Dave's death, the resilience of youth she thought. But they needed the break as well. It had been an impulsive move but a necessary one.

Anne had first seen the advertisement in one of her glossies. 'Get away from it all', was the headline, which was the forerunner of paradise. A small cottage, recently refurbished, in a secluded wood on the South Downs. Well off the beaten track.

Well, this was well off the beaten track all right. Although it should only have taken about two hours driving to get from suburbia to here she had been driving for the better part of four, thanks to a few wrong turnings, before she saw the turning listed in the travel agents brochure. She had driven about three miles from there along a road which had become steadily worse, until it could only be described as a track. A rutted, pitted, dried out mud track and there was still no sign of any cottage.

All of a sudden, the car entered the clearing. The woods stopped at a well-manicured lawn, which ran up to an idyllic looking cottage, behind which the woods started up again.

Anne pulled to a halt, and all got out, herself and Elizabeth to stretch limbs long gone to sleep and the twins to charge off, nearly missing the admonition not to go too far.

Elizabeth fished around in the glove box and found the key, which they had picked up from the Travel Agent. "Let's go and see if it fits," she said sardonically.

"Leave the bags for now, honey, we'll have a nose around first, sort them out later."

"Suits me," replied Elizabeth.

Magically, the key did fit and they let themselves into a narrow hallway with doors leading both left and right.

They opened the first door and entered into a small kitchen. Everything had a neat, well-finished appearance and a cursory inspection revealed that it had most of the mod cons.

"I was half afraid that we'd be getting water from a well in the back yard or some such."

"Don't exaggerate mother," Elizabeth sighed, eyes heavenward, "the Travel Agent said it was kitted out recently. Strikes me as we have everything we need right here."

They continued their tour of the cottage, revealing a bathroom next door, three bedrooms upstairs, and finally the living room.

Up until then they had been pleasantly surprised. Hot and cold running water, a bath, and an indoor toilet. Nowhere near as back to nature as either had secretly feared.

However, they both stood in shock in the doorway as they looked across the living room to the far wall.

"Oh, great," whispered Elizabeth dramatically, "the Munsters' fireplace."

"It does look a trifle...uh...gothic," Anne said shivering slightly.

The object of their trepidation was truly grotesque.

A massive fireplace, far too large for the room, stood opposite them. The mantelpiece was held up by two columns, at the base of which were carved wolves. Their mouths open, tongues lolling, eyes the kind that follow you around the room. Coiling up the columns it seemed that flames chased poor tormented souls, whose agony was carved into the stone for all eternity. None looking the same, but all having a look of pure horror. The worst of this ill aspected feature, however, was around the fire itself. A demonic looking character leered at them. His stone arms reaching out and down until they met the edge of the fire. Here, each of his hands were curled around another soul, terror-etching features.

The twins raced past and squatted directly on the hearth.

"It's lovely."

"It's brilliant."

They screamed in unison.

"It's ghastly," Anne turned away, revulsion evident in the set of her face.

20

"It'll look far better when the fire's lit, they always look homely," ventured Elizabeth, though not with any great conviction. Secretly she was quite drawn to the fireplace, although she couldn't think why.

"Let's get unpacked and I'll fix us a bite to eat," Anne suggested. "OK, mother," but for some reason Elizabeth couldn't tear herself away from the fireplace.

The twins didn't even acknowledge her, just kept staring at the demonic figure as he seemed to squeeze the last vestiges of sanity from his captured souls.

"I'm not going to do it myself," stated Anne.

"Uh?"

"The unpacking. I could do with some help?"

"Oh yeah, of course. Come on weasels, let's get our stuff from the car." The twins, however, remained transfixed. "It's no use ma, this looks like a job for me and you."

"Come on then number one daughter, the sooner we start, the sooner we're finished."

*

It was dusk by the time Anne and Elizabeth had unpacked all their gear, got the twins fed and watered and put to bed. They relaxed after eating their own meals with a glass of wine each.

Anne lit a cigarette and leaned back in her chair. "How do you feel?" she asked, stretching out her legs.

"OK I guess. It's nice to be away from all the hustle and bustle, but...I miss dad."

"I know honey, I do too. He would have liked it here."

"Yeah."

"Fancy a quick turn around the garden before we close up for the night?"

Elizabeth thought for a moment and then shrugged, "OK, I guess I am pretty tired."

They walked out into the darkening clearing and looked up at the stars.

"It's pretty spooky."

"What is?" Anne questioned, her mind momentarily elsewhere. Brought from her reverie she could only think of the remoteness of their cottage. "I like it, miles from any interference, we can just stay here a few weeks and get ourselves together. Besides, there's a family not too far from here. Apparently they look after this place and if we have any problems we can just go and see them."

"No, I mean the fireplace. Can't seem to get it out of my mind. It's kind of horrible, but attractive. Do you know how I mean?"

Anne thought of her first boyfriend for a moment, "Horrible and attractive huh? Yes I suppose I do. Why don't you go to bed honey?"

"Yeah, I will. Goodnight."

"Goodnight."

Elizabeth ambled back to the cottage, tired but still thinking about the fireplace. She looked back to see if her mother had moved, but she was still stargazing. Smiling to herself, Elizabeth climbed the stairs to the room she had chosen and turned in.

*

The man continued to watch the older woman as the young lady entered the cottage.

He had watched them arrive, the two who had consumed his attention just now and the two girls, probably about eight years old, not that he was any judge. "Perfect," he thought to himself. Perfect.

He continued to watch the older woman. She seemed sad. He would find out why and, if necessary, use the knowledge.

Mustn't rush it though. No. If any of his training had taught him anything it was to plan, wait until you are certain and then plan again.

He would plan. Plan and wait.

He could afford to wait; they could all afford to wait. Time was something which was most definitely on their side.

He watched until the older lady had gone back into the cottage. It wasn't until minutes later, after the lights had gone out, that he rose from his hiding place and left.

*

Anne woke with a start. Looking over at her clock the illuminated dial said 03:21; apart from this glow the room was pitch black.

Had she heard a noise? - she wasn't sure. After a moment's disorientation where she couldn't place her surroundings, it came to her. She was in the cottage and someone was moving around downstairs.

Without thinking, she crossed the bedroom floor and opened the door to the landing. This had always been Dave's job. He would investigate the strange noises or laugh and tell her it was the boiler, or the stairs contracting after the heat of the day. He always chased any fears away. But she had always been easily scared. Especially when Dave had been away. Checking that each door had been locked at least three times before going to bed. It wasn't a fear of vampires or ghosts, but living on the outskirts of a major city where

23

even a cursory inspection of the newspapers told you that there were a lot of nasty people in this world. There was only her, she must put aside any fears of her own and think of the children. Creeping downstairs, her sleep-fogged mind suddenly realized that she wasn't best equipped for a confrontation.

Clad only in an oversize t-shirt she darted into the kitchen and grabbed a sharp knife.

Soft muted sounds came from the living room. She headed over to the door which was ajar and looked through.

Seated in front of the fireplace were the twins. Both were gazing at the dying embers of the small fire she had lit earlier to ward off the evening's chill.

Neither moved - they appeared mesmerized by the flicker of the last embers.

Feeling a trifle foolish wearing a t-shirt and holding a large bread knife, Anne flung the door wide.

"Victoria...Mary, get to bed this instant!" Her feeling of foolishness made her voice shrill.

The twins, snapped from their vigil, jumped to their feet and darted past her, on their way back to bed. If either saw the knife they were wise enough not to mention it.

Anne followed after checking the front door was still locked. "Doesn't hurt to make certain," she muttered under her breath.

Unseen by both Anne and her siblings, Elizabeth emerged from the shadows behind the living-room door. Quietly moving to her sisters' former position in front of the fire, she knelt.

Although she couldn't begin to think why, the fireplace was so grotesque, she felt calm here. It was as if she belonged. Not like at home where she had always felt that no one understood her, or thought her freaky because she was aloof, like at school. Right here, right now, in front of the fireplace she felt completely at ease for the first time since her father had died.

It had been difficult sleeping upstairs, too quiet, she thought after a moment. She was used to the unceasing noise of a town. With no one around for a good mile she had thought she would feel scared, all alone. But it was weird, kneeling in front of the fireplace, she felt at home.

It was nearing dawn when she woke, thoroughly refreshed, even though she had slept on the rug next to the hearth.

A pale grey light was beginning to come through the windows and she sat up. Looking once again into the fire, completely dead now.

Or was it? Clinging to life in the chimney just within view was a last glow. As she looked it appeared to get brighter before it too disappeared.

All thoughts of the fireplace looking horrible had gone.

Chapter 2

As Anne woke the sun outside her window had just begun to clear the trees around the clearing.

She had slept for hours, but still felt tense.

She dressed quickly and went downstairs. The twins were already up, sitting on the rug in front of the hearth.

"Breakfast?" she asked.

"Lizzie made us some before she went out."

"Went out where?"

"Don't know."

"OK." Anne wasn't overly concerned. Elizabeth was old enough to look after herself. Besides, she probably needed time on her own.

Grabbing her cigarettes on her way out, Anne went to sit on the lawn. It had the look of a nice day.

She screamed when she saw the remains on the doorstep.

The twins came running.

"What is it?" asked Victoria.

"I think it was a squirrel." After the initial shock of seeing the torn little body, Anne's calm was beginning to reassert itself.

"Aah. Poor little thing," said the twins in unison.

"Probably left there by a cat or something, you two go back inside, I'll clean this up." Gingerly picking the remains up by the tail she threw it in the dustbin. Then back inside to quickly wash her hands, whilst not normally squeamish, Anne didn't relish this sort of thing.

Any thoughts of breakfast had disappeared with her grisly discovery.

"Come on kids. Let's go and introduce ourselves to the Holmans."

"Who?"

"The Holmans are like caretakers of this place. It's only polite to let them know we're here."

*

Elizabeth had set off with no idea of where she was going. She felt full of life, she strolled along, not a care in the world. Stopping to kneel and give close inspection to an attractive flower now and again. She wished she knew some of their names. So tiny and beautiful, the smells so delicate.

Even though it wasn't quiet here she revelled in the peace of the setting. Birds singing, the drone of a bee somewhere off to the left. She sat at the base of an enormous tree and stretched out her legs.

Leaning back between the massive roots, she sighed. Her thoughts turned back to her father. She missed him. It seemed that of all the people in the world he had been there for her. Not that that was strictly true, since his job took him away for long periods at a time. But he was always laughing and joking, taking her fears away.

She felt guilty about her walk now. She had forgotten him. Although she knew that she wouldn't be able to keep him at the forefront of her mind all the time, she felt bad. It was as if she had let him down. She was sure that he would be the first person to tell her to get on with her life, that was small comfort. The wound left by his passing was too new, too raw.

She wondered how she could have forgotten. Last night she had had the best night's sleep in weeks since he'd gone. Strange, all those nights in her own bed, staring at the ceiling. Now the first night in a strange house and she'd slept on the living-room floor. Odd.

She continued indulging herself in memories of her father, letting the bees and birds continue their work around her.

Gradually another sound began to invade her senses. A kind of rythmical chopping. She got slowly to her feet, her feelings of peace driven out by the noise but swiftly replaced by a burning curiosity.

She made her way towards the sound along a narrow path. The woods here began to thicken and the light to dim. Shafts of sunlight still broke through the canopy alive with dustmotes and midges, the light in between suffused with a green hue.

The sound grew louder and as she approached, the path widened into a small clearing. Stopping just short of it, Elizabeth had a sudden feeling of wrongness. Nothing she could put a finger on. But her curiosity pushed it all to one side. Moving to a tree at the very edge of the clearing she glanced round and gasped at the sight in front of her.

In the centre of the clearing next to a small woodpile stood a man. Not just any man. He was gorgeous. Stripped to the waist, his muscley back was covered in a sheen of sweat. His hair, a dark blonde, curled down around his ears. His perspiration making it curlier, darker. As he stretched upwards she could see he was tall but his broad shoulders made it less noticeable. Whilst he didn't have the six pack stomach that her pop idols all strived for he was far from being fat. It was solid muscle rather than that contrived through a gym. With powerful downstrokes of his axe the woodpile was slowly growing larger.

She stood transfixed. The girls at school would turn green with envy when they heard about this.

He turned and looked straight at her, how could he have realized she was there?

"Good morning," he offered.

"Oh... Hi. I'm sorry, I didn't mean to interrupt you."

"No problem. You at the old cottage?"

"Yeah. I got here yesterday."

"You must be Elizabeth?" Without waiting for the affirmation, he propped his axe against the woodpile and strode easily towards her, his hand stretched out towards her. "The name's Geoff. I sorta look after this wood and your cottage."

He shook her hand warmly. She felt a thrill at his touch. It was like an electric shock. She felt hot inside, and could not look away from his deep green eyes.

"Everything OK?"

"Yeah," she replied a little breathless. "I'm not really used to all this fresh air."

"I meant the cottage."

She felt stupid, her cheeks hot, she started to stammer about how lovely the cottage was.

He smiled at her, "Fancy a beer?"

"Guess so."

He leaned over the woodpile and retrieved a couple of cans, passing one to her.

It was cool.

She fumbled the ring pull and again felt embarassed. Taking a long draught, she started to feel a little giddy. Why? She'd drunk beer before, admittedly it wasn't all the time, but she wasn't a stranger to strong drink. She looked up from the can to find his eyes upon her.

"Nice?"

"Yeah...very." She couldn't quite think properly. After a moment she realized that it wasn't just the beer. It was him. He was making her heart beat overtime.

"Another?"

"I shouldn't, I don't want to stop you from your work." What a total load of rubbish. The last thing she wanted was for him to go. "But if you don't mind."

"Here." This time he opened the can for her. He had seen her fumbling the first. She coloured again. Christ, how awkward she was feeling.

She suddenly realized that he was waiting for an answer. "Sorry, I didn't hear what you said." She felt herself melting into his eyes.

"It's OK, I just said that I'd bring some wood round later this afternoon for your fire. It can get kinda chilly in the evenings round here. Weather gets mixed up this time of year. Starts off looking like the most glorious day of your life, next thing you're wading through a foot of water."

"Mmm." God she couldn't even string a sentence together now. Torn between wanting to run back to the cottage before she put him off speaking to her altogether and wanting him to put his arms around her and stay forever, she stood, choosing the former.

Whilst not a novice where men were concerned, she had only ever had one boyfriend and Geoff the dreamy woodcutter looked like he knew more than Spencer the spotty fumbler who had developed at least ten pairs of hands when she had babysat with him that time, and although he had wanted to, she had stopped him before it went any further. Stopped him and never seen him again.

"Can I see you again?" She felt herself reddening once more. Two cans of beer and she was being as forward as some of the girls at school she despised for doing exactly that. But she knew that this was different. Geoff was a real man.

"Of course, I'll be bringing the wood round later," he smiled. "Besides I'm always here or hereabouts. Should see quite a bit of each other."

Her heart leapt and hammered in her breast. Trying to appear nonchalant she coolly said, "Look forward to it."

She didn't so much walk as float across the clearing. Behind her she heard him begin chopping again. Looking round for one final glimpse to savour, he turned at that precise moment and waved. Feeling guilty, she returned the wave and hurried to the seclusion of the surrounding wood.

Daydreaming all the way she walked slowly back to the cottage. She dragged her heels all the way, not hurrying to get back, for then real life would push her thoughts of Geoff away.

*

Anne was armed with a sketch map of the woods and some of the pathways through them. It was becoming evident after a while that her map wasn't quite as exact as she might have liked.

She was lost.

The twins were charging through the brush around her keeping mostly in sight. She turned and tried to peer through the trees in the vain hope that she could see something which looked remotely like the Holmans' cottage. So far nothing.

Should she backtrack? She supposed that she would have to.

"Victoria... Mary," she called, "Back here now, we're going back home."

No answer.

She realized that she couldn't even hear them anymore.

She called again. Louder this time.

Again no answer.

Where had she last seen them? She couldn't think. Fighting the rising panic she called again, "Vicky... Mary!" Was this part of one of their games? It could be, but even so, if she was lost the chance that they could get lost was fairly evident.

Further along the path, half hidden by interposing trees she saw a movement and hurried towards it.

"Mary, Victoria! Get back here this instant!" Now that she could see her goal, anger quickly took over the panic. Already in the back of her mind she was preparing the tongue-lashing she was about to unleash.

These thoughts scattered as she ran full pelt round a bend in the path and crashed into the man coming in the other direction. He made a valiant attempt to catch her, but her impetus carried her onward until she fell, full stretch, face down and skidded into a bush bordering the path.

In an instant the man was beside her.

"Are you alright?"

She looked up, straight into his eyes and gasped. He was certainly an attractive man. Kind of film star looks, deep blue eyes, chiselled jaw.

"Are you alright?" he repeated.

"Yes, I feel a trifle foolish stuck in this bush here, but nothing broken, except my pride."

He smiled and helped her to her feet. "I guess you must be Mrs. Masterson? I'm Geoff Holman," he shook her hand.

"Very nice," she thought to herself, "yes, call me Anne please."

"Pleased to meet you Anne." He smiled again, revealing perfect white teeth.

She gazed at him a moment longer and then thinking that he might think her rude, quickly said, "I was just on my way to see Mr. and Mrs. Holman." She left it as a question, not quite sure who she was addressing. "That's my mother and father, but you won't find them here. You need to go back down this trail about half a mile, the path forks there, you need the left-hand path. Takes you straight to the front door."

Anne caught herself suddenly. What was she thinking of, eyeing this man up? The twins.

"My daughters, I was looking for them." How could she have forgotten?

"What's the matter? Have they been gone long?" His face was a picture of concern. "Where did you see them last?"

"Back down the path, they were playing in the woods and I lost sight of them."

"Don't worry, my father's out at the moment, they might be with him. Let's see if we can't get them back for you."

She looked at him, he didn't seem too worried, and the reassuring smile he gave her made her feel at ease.

He turned to retrieve a hand-cart piled high with logs that she hadn't even noticed. "Come on then," he held out his hand and unthinking she took it.

They walked back down the path to where she thought she had last seen her children. He smiled and chatted amiably with her, making sure that everything in the cottage was to her liking.

"Everything is perfect, it's such a lovely setting, so peaceful. Just what we needed, you know, to get away from everything," Anne complimented him. "Although the fireplace may take a bit of getting used to." Understatement of the century she thought to herself, the fact was it gave her the creeps. In the cold light of day she was sure that was why she had over-reacted the previous night.

"Ah, yes, the fireplace. It's the only original feature you know, one of the reasons that we kept it when we rebuilt everything was because of the legend," Geoff said dramatically. She looked at him to see if he appeared as B-movie horror as he sounded.

"What legend?" she scoffed, was this the ghost story that would be used to attract future holidaymakers to come and visit the cottage? Some macabre tale to titivate a gullible public, like some stately home with a headless former resident.

"Well, a few hundred years ago, it seems that a witch lived here, she murdered a couple of kids, you know, cut their hearts out, that kind of thing. Anyway the locals cornered her in the cottage and somehow or another she was burned alive, took quite a bit of the cottage with her, but the fireplace was undamaged. Seems it was her altar or somesuch." He looked at her disbelieving face and laughed. "It's a true story, although I must confess that my mother tells it better."

Anne arched an eyebrow at him and his story, "Very spooky I'm sure."

He stopped and looked directly into her eyes, she could think of nothing else. "You shouldn't mock, things used to happen around here back in the old days."

He was so compelling, so beautiful. Abruptly he turned and pointed. "The missing children I believe."

She looked past him and sure enough, crouching down with an old man, there they were. The spell broke, it was like the sun suddenly appearing on a cloudy day. She felt a shiver down her spine, but this was forgotten in the joy of being reunited with the children. She started to run to them but Geoff grabbed her arm. She spun on him angrily.

"Wait, don't disturb them yet. Look."

She turned again and peered at the three crouching down in the bushes. They had something between them. The old man was talking to the children who nodded excitedly. He looked up and saw Anne and Geoff standing someway off. First raising a finger to his lips he beckoned them over.

Anne looked at Geoff, the query evident in her eyes.

"It's OK, it's my father," he explained. "Come on, but keep quiet." So saying he approached the group.

Anne followed certain that something was happening, but not sure what. The thing between her children and the elder Holman turned at the noise she made as she walked towards it.

It was a young deer! It was beautiful!

She hurried over, but in doing so startled the young creature. In an instant it was on it's feet and bounded off into the wood.

The children looked to see what had scared the fawn and in doing, ruined their treasured moment. Their eyes fixed accusingly on their mother.

Anne spread her hands, "I'm sorry," she stammered.

The elder Holman stood, "Doesn't matter, doesn't do them much good to have too much contact with humans," it was offered more as an olive branch than a quicky guide to simple woodcraft, she knew, but she still felt like a naughty schoolgirl.

After all the introductions had been made and Anne had reasserted herself, George Holman, as it turned out the father's name, offered to walk Anne and the children back to his own home to meet, as he called her "the wife."

Geoff caught up with Anne before she left. "I'm going to take all this wood to your cottage first, did you want for me to light you a fire? Ward off any chill that the evening might bring?" he offered.

Anne found that whenever he seemed to be speaking of such mundane things she couldn't think straight. It was as if he had some hold over her. She shook herself, it wasn't as if he was that good looking.

"Uh... yeah... OK, that'd be nice."

"Right, hope to see you again soon?" He left it as a question. She nodded dumbly and he set off pulling his cart behind him.

. As if released from a spell, her thoughts came rushing back. Elizabeth. She'd been out most of the day. Was she alright?

Dave. For the first time since his death she hadn't thought about him. Strange. Her psychiatrist had said that she would, eventually, get over the loss of her husband, but in a little over a month? She felt guilt well up inside her. The first time she'd come across a handsome man, she'd forgotten her husband. The fact that nothing whatsoever had occured couldn't banish the feelings of betrayal that threatened to choke her.

"Mrs. Masterson?"

She looked up, fighting back tears.

"Are you alright ma'am?"

"Yes. Yes, I'm fine."

"Well, as you like." George Holman looked unconvinced. "No point standing around all day, the wife'll put a brew on for us. No better cook than the wife, and that's a fact. See if'n she can't rustle us all up a bit of dinner."

So saying he turned, stretching a hand out to each of her children which they grasped eagerly, and set off.

Trailing along behind, her confused emotions warring within her, her children laughing as they chatted to the old man, Anne felt slightly amused.

Chapter 3

Anne woke early the next morning and groaned. Her body felt massive and bloated. She sat up in bed and tried to think why. Rubbing her eyes with the palms of her hands it all came back to her. Mrs. Holman's cooking.

Mrs. Holman, if she had a first name it had never been mentioned, had proved to be one of those larger matronly type women. The kind who look you up and down as if gauging how much food you'll need to eat before you are healthy. This had led from the snack she had originally started preparing turning into a virtual banquet.

Anne tried not to think badly of her, it was obviously her nature, besides it was difficult to think badly of anyone who could cook like Mrs. Holman. Vast mountains of food had been created seemingly from nothing and Anne had found herself eating more than she would ever have thought possible. The woman was a saint.

The twins had eaten far more cakes and homemade sweetmeats than Anne thought was good for them, but every protest had been kindly turned aside by Mrs. Holman with, "Don't worry yourself dear, children can always find a bit more room for one of my cakes." After a while it had become obvious that her protests were in vain and Anne gave into Mrs. Holman, realising that she was fighting a losing battle.

Anne had been used to cooking with vegetable oil, light salads and all the other more modern trends in cooking. Mrs. Holman was a cook of the old style. This wasn't a criticism, but Anne's body was full to the brim of 'proper' food and had to get used to digesting it again.

But it had been so delicious.

Dragging herself out of bed, she showered and went downstairs to make herself a cup of coffee. Taking it through to the living room she sat down on the settee. Since it was still early morning she felt a definite chill and leaned over to stoke the fire. The last embers were still red so she added a couple of logs. Instantly a red flame jumped onto them and the fire, as far as she was concerned, was lit. Even if it didn't last, at least it would warm the room up a bit before the kids came down.

She grabbed up her cigarettes and lighter and went outside. It was not full light, the sun hadn't cleared the trees, but it felt cool and fresh. She lit up and drank her coffee.

Sitting down on the grass she pulled her knees up and cradled them with her arms. She began to feel damp from the dew soaking through her dressing-gown, but she didn't mind. The birds were singing, the day was fresh, she felt clean. It was lovely.

Slowly another feeling began to push out her calm reverie. She was being watched. It wasn't an instant recognition, it was a slow dawning. Someone was watching her. Turning her head quickly she looked up at the house, half expecting to see one of the girls at the window. But there was no-one there. She scanned the surrounding tree-line, but with the sun just appearing the trees were just so much shadow.

Suppressing a quick shiver that had nothing to do with the early morning chill she stood and hurried back into the house, shutting the door firmly behind her.

Elizabeth stood there already dressed.

"Are you alright mum?" she enquired part concerned, part amused. A half smile playing at the corners of her mouth.

"Yes, of course I am. Why shouldn't I be?" Anne's response was quite tart.

"No reason, you just seemed in a bit of a hurry."

"I was getting cold."

"OK. Fancy a cuppa?"

"Yeah, OK. What do you fancy doing today, any plans?"

"Not really, thought I might take a stroll, but nothing concrete. Ya know."

"Well Mr. Holman said he'd come over and take us all out for a ramble, perhaps have a picnic? Make a day of it. What do you think?"

"No, I'll stick around here, maybe go out later."

"Come on," pleaded Anne, "It'll be nice, the four of us. It'll be fun."

Fun was exactly the opposite of what Elizabeth thought of the idea, but she couldn't tell her mother that. Not without hurting her feelings. Fun would be seeing if Geoff was in the woods again. That would be nice.

"No, you go and enjoy yourselves. I don't really fancy it."

"OK, but don't go too far on your own," at the back of Anne's mind was the feeling of being watched, and although it was probably nothing, it didn't hurt to be careful.

"No, I won't," Elizabeth promised, "what time were you thinking of going anyway?"

"Nothing specific, but I get the feeling that the Holmans are early risers," Anne's eyes rolled skywards, "so I had best see about getting the twins up."

"They are already, I saw them go into the living room before you came in."

"Are you sure? I thought they'd be in bed ages yet."

So saying, Anne opened the living room door and sure enough the twins were seated in front of the fire, exchanging one of their private looks that Anne had realised long ago, meant they were talking to each other. Not talking as such, since they didn't actually say anything aloud, but they certainly knew what the other was thinking. These moments excluded everyone else and they could be quite stroppy if interrupted. But Anne needed them ready for their day out, so she bit the proverbial bullet and went in.

Surprisingly, they were fine, once Anne had explained herself, and they tore upstairs to get dressed while Anne made them their breakfast.

*

Elizabeth had a day to plan. Mr. Holman had turned up early, but everyone had been ready and although her mother had tried once more to persuade her to go, she had managed to fend her off.

All she could really think of was meeting with Geoff again. But this time it would be different. This time she resolved not to flounder or get embarrassed. This time she was going to be the picture of serenity.

But she wasn't going to rush out. She spent the early part of the morning showering and making sure that she looked perfect. Not that she was going to glide through the woods in a ballgown, well not quite. She had chosen her cotton dress which she thought did flatter her. Showing her figure off in a good way, but not tarty. She wanted to get the right mix of femininity but not girly. It was floral, but in a rural way she decided, not at all prissy.

She looked critically at herself in her bedroom mirror, turning this way and that until she was certain that her ensemble was perfect.

When she was at last satisfied, she went downstairs and pinching a couple of her mother's ciggies, she went out into the glade. Pausing only to light one, she set off into the woods.

As on the previous day, Elizabeth took delight in her surroundings. The birds were singing, butterflies in a myriad of colours flitted from bush to bush suddenly caught in a shaft of sunlight, their beauty breathtaking. Every now and again a squirrel would stop on the path in front of her, not so much scared as wary, curious as it's beady eyes would look at her. Each time she would stop and wait until at the last, almost too quick to see, it would be off, a red blur and it was halfway up a tree. Rabbits too in abundance. It was almost like a scene from a child's fairytale. Elizabeth imagined that if she stayed any longer, songbirds would alight upon her upraised palms and trill to her.

She approached the tree where she had paused the day before and as if a trigger to her memory, thoughts of her father came flooding in. Seeing no sense in rushing things she halted again and sat once more in the trees roots. It was a truly lovely place to sit and contemplate she thought. Not quiet, not with the sounds of all the wildlife, but peaceful all the same.

Her thoughts full of memories of times spent with her father abounded and she gave herself over to them. Everything else forgotten for now. Elizabeth relived days at the beach when she was younger, bike rides, picnics, days out, all the lovely times she could remember spending with him. Interspersed with more mundane memories of him coming home unexpectedly from work and picking her up, swinging her round.

Elizabeth's reverie became a doze. Not fully asleep, but right at that point where she was no longer quite awake. The tranquillity of the setting encouraging her to relax more than she had intended. As she progressed closer towards sleep, her memories of her father changed abruptly. A white light blotted out the images which had been gently wending their way through her mind. It was a mental jolt, but of itself not enough to make her fully awake. Elizabeth wasn't afraid because somehow she knew that the white light was linked to her father. She didn't know how or why. She just knew.

Then as if from far, far away she heard her father's voice, too distant to make out any words. She felt warm inside. Her father was with her, with this thought she came fully awake. All in all, it had probably only lasted a minute, maybe less, but it was enough. Filled to bursting with a sense of well-being, she stood and stretched. Straightening her dress she continued with her journey to see Geoff.

What a glorious day.

*

Mr Holman had called for Anne and the twins at eight o'clock. As luck would have it, the twins had eaten their breakfast and gotten dressed without too much hassle. Because she had spent her morning sorting them out, Anne had not had a chance to eat herself, but not wishing to keep Mr. Holman waiting, she had left without bothering to eat. At first this hadn't bothered her, but as the morning had gone on Anne began to feel hungrier and hungrier. The empty space in her growling stomach was beginning to make her short-tempered. Not that anyone noticed. The twins were totally engrossed in Mr. Holman's narrative.

To be fair, Mr. Holman knew his stuff. He had pointed out things of interest throughout the morning. Ever since leaving the cottage when they had been shown how to identify the spoor of a fox, tracking it from where it had sat in the clearing for at least a mile through the woods. He had an obvious love for the countryside and his enthusiasm rubbed off on Victoria and Mary.

Every bird, butterfly, beetle, Mr. Holman knew their names, where they lived, what they did and how and why they did it. Similarly, all of the surrounding foliage was introduced. The man truly was a font of knowledge.

Despite her early cynicism Anne too was slowly won over, and the rest of the morning flew past. So it was that Anne was pleasantly surprised when their walk took them into a small clearing where Mrs. Holman had spread a blanket out on the ground and was busily unpacking a picnic.

Mrs. Holman looked up and called them over, "Come on, help yourselves, there's plenty of everything."

And she was right, although the blanket was quite large it was quickly filled with food. Cold meats, salad, bowls of crisps, sandwiches, cakes and biscuits. Food enough for all of them and a few others besides thought Anne as she started to fill her plate.

The food, as Anne had expected, was delicious. But as with all delicious food, she overate and when Mr. Holman announced his intention to continue with the nature trail Anne had to cry off. She felt bloated.

The twins, however, were having none of it.

"Please, mummy, please let us stay!" they chorused.

Anne was nonplussed. Victoria and Mary never sought anyone's company. They were always too busy with one another. Their games were always to the exclusion of everyone else. Now, however, they wanted to carry on with Mr. Holman, a man they had only met yesterday. Sometimes Anne thought she would never understand them. This was one such time.

During the momentary lapse when Anne's mind tried to take this sudden behavioural change on board, Mr. Holman spoke up. "Don't mind taking them off you for the afternoon, if that's alright by you?"

"No I couldn't ask you to, it wouldn't be fair," Anne protested albeit half-heartedly.

"Truth to tell, I am quite enjoying myself," the old man's weathered face broke into a smile. "Takes me back a few years, having children around again, ya know," he chuckled.

Mrs. Holman added her four pennies worth. "Let George take 'em, they'll be OK. Me and you can go back to the cottage and have a nice cuppa."

Throughout this exchange Victoria and Mary had been chanting that plaintive "please" that always grates on an adult's nerves. This more than anything else (although if she was honest, trekking around the woods this morning had quite worn her out) made her relent. With all the troubles of the last couple of months it would be nice for them to get out and enjoy themselves (again, if she was completely honest, if she'd said no they would have driven her mad in the cottage that afternoon). No, all things considered, thought Anne, it would be best all round. With this she acquiesced.

"OK, but no annoying Mr. Holman," she cautioned, "Are you sure you don't mind?" This last was directed to the old man.

"No, it'll be a pleasure. Back around teatime, OK?"

"Fine."

So off they went leaving Anne and Mrs. Holman to tidy up and cart everything back home.

*

Elizabeth paused at the edge of the clearing peering around through the trees. There was no sign of Geoff. Swallowing her disappointment she leaned further around the tree straining to get a clearer view.

All of a sudden, a hand touched her shoulder. Elizabeth felt her heart smash through her ribcage. Falling forward, she lost her balance and fell heavily to her hands and knees. "Everything OK?"

Elizabeth spun around and ended up half sprawled, half sitting on the floor looking up at Geoff. His concern thinly veiling his obvious amusement at her ridiculous predicament.

Jumping to her feet and smoothing her dress down Elizabeth could have died with embarrassment.

"I am fine, you startled me, that's all," she stammered cursing herself mentally, this wasn't going to plan at all. She was supposed to be alluring.

"You are not chopping wood," she stated. Marvellous, she thought. State the obvious.

"No, I was just about to start, but I saw you and thought I'd say hello," he replied.

Something didn't quite add up. He was coming from her cottage... then he smiled and the thought was gone.

"Fancy a walk?" he offered.

"Yes." Elizabeth upbraided herself again. Too quick. Got to be a bit more laid back, not disinterested, but not all over him like a rash. "Yeah, that would be nice." Much better, she congratulated herself. If anything Geoff's smile grew broader, but he offered his hand and Elizabeth took it. Strolling through the woods, he was perfectly at ease and she began to feel more comfortable, less awkward with his presence.

After a few minutes Elizabeth found herself thinking of her father, perhaps because she had daydreamed about him earlier.

Geoff listened, but didn't offer any comment. She told him of his illness, what he had meant to her. But stopped short of telling him of the dream, it was too recent.

As she spoke, Geoff put his arm around her shoulder, encouraging her to speak on, and she found herself telling him more and more.

*

Mary looked over at Victoria and they shared one of their private looks. The kind which meant nothing to anyone else, but could speak a thousand words between each other. This look simply said "Brilliant!"

Mr. Holman had elected, or been elected, it didn't matter to them which, to take the girls on a journey of exploration through the woods. It was superb, there wasn't a tree, bird, plant or bug that Mr. Holman didn't recognise instantly. Pointing out objects of interest virtually at every step.

He told them all he could in the time allotted, but both were hungry for more.

"How much more?" he had asked.

"Everything," they had both replied.

That was why now they were all walking deeper and deeper into the woods. Mr. Holman leading, the twins following, hand in hand.

As the woods around them got thicker, the sunlight grew more strangled, until it had all but disappeared, leaving them to trail Mr. Holman into an ever gloomier part of the wood.

Far from feeling any fear, the twins felt thrilled. Here, finally, was an adult who was prepared to show them interesting things, not just shout at them and tell them what not to do.

Abruptly, Mr. Holman stopped. Turning he said, "What I am about to show you must remain a secret between us three, agreed?"

They nodded.

Mr. Holman spat into his hand and thrust it towards the twins. They returned the compliment and shook hands solemnly. This was a pact.

"Right then," he started, "A long time ago there was a beautiful princess who lived around here. She got herself lost in these woods and would have died, but after days of wandering around a wolf found her and took her safely to the nearest village."

"But I thought wolves killed people," interrupted Victoria.

"No. No, wolves are good creatures, men kill wolves, not the other way 'round. Now where'd I get to?"

"The wolf took her to the village," reminded Mary.

"Ah, yes, that's right. Well the villagers were simple folk, they saw the princess there all ragged from living in the woods standing with a wolf and they thought she was a witch." He paused and looked at each of the twins, "And you know what they did to witches in the olden days don't you?"

They shook their heads, Mary's hand came up to her mouth.

"They burned her alive. Killed the wolf as well."

"How cruel!"

"Yes, but that's not the end of the story. Because she was killed so cruelly, the princess' spirit cannot rest. She roams the woods, the only things that will allow her to rest for a while is animals."

"How?" asked Mary.

"That's even sadder girls, the animals have to die as well and be burned like she was."

"Uh. How awful!"

"That's the truth of it right enough," agreed Mr. Holman, "but what are we supposed to do? She needs a rest doesn't she?"

47

Sharing another look the girls agreed.

"Can we help?"

"Well now, I suppose you could. But you'd have to keep it secret."

Victoria and Mary spat into their hands without hesitation, "What do you want us to do?"

Pausing only to sit upon a fallen log, Mr. Holman told them exactly what they needed to know.

*

Anne had returned home in the mid afternoon to find the cottage empty. Elizabeth must still be out, she thought to herself, not unduly worried, she knew that Dave's death had hit her quite badly and that perhaps a bit of time on her own would do her good.

She pottered around for a bit, tidied the twins' room and went for a sit down in the living room. But the fireplace oppressed her and she felt uncomfortable. Ghastly thing, she thought to herself. The fire in the hearth flamed momentarily as if in answer.

Getting up, Anne noticed that evening was drawning in and as she stood, she heard the twins returning. Moving towards the door it suddenly burst open and the twins charged past her. No acknowledgement, no hello mum, nothing. They just disappeared into the living room. Anne raised her eyes heavenwards and shrugged.

"Hope I'm not too late?" Mr. Holman spoke from the doorway.

"No," Anne sighed, "not at all, thank you for taking the time with them."

"Thoroughly enjoyed myself if I'm honest."

"Mummy can we go again tomorrow?" Victoria shouted from the doorway of the living room.

"No, I'm sure Mr. Holman must be busy," and even if he wasn't, Anne would have liked to spend a bit of time with them herself.

"I'd like to, if it doesn't interfere with anything you might be doing?" Mr. Holman interjected.

"I really couldn't impose on you further Mr. Holman."

"No imposition dear, shall we say eight o'clock again?"

"Please mummy," chorused the twins.

What the hell thought Anne. But instead just said "OK."

"Tomorrow it is then, bye for now," Mr. Holman confirmed and turned for home.

"Yes, bye," Anne turned to speak to the girls, but they had gone, following them to the living room she watched as they sat and stared into the flames. Shaking her head she went and started their tea.

*

It was getting close to full dark by the time Elizabeth returned home. She had wandered around the woods with him all day, talking, sometimes he would offer something of his own, but mostly she spoke. Telling him of herself. It had truly been a lovely day.

It ended as she opened the door to the cottage. "Shall I see you again tomorrow?" she asked.

"Yes, I'll be about."

She turned the handle and as she pushed the door her mother was there.

"Where the hell have you been?" Anne stormed, "I've been worried sick!"

"I went for a walk, I told you I was," Elizabeth defended herself, devastated that Geoff was witnessing this.

"Inside, now, young lady."

"Why, I was only..."

"Inside!"

Elizabeth ran up the stairs, nearly crying with embarrassment.

"I'm sorry if I've caused any trouble, Mrs. Masterson. I didn't realise she had to be home at any given time."

Anne spun round from watching Elizabeth leave, she'd totally forgotten Geoff was even there.

"Please don't apologise, that girl could try the patience of a Saint sometime, it's me that should apologise to you. Has she made a nuisance of herself?"

"No, not at all, we've had a nice chat, she's a very pleasant young lady," Geoff smiled.

Anne's eyebrows arched at the statement, but his smile robbed her of any worries.

Chapter 4

It was fully dark by the time that Anne started the short journey home. Mrs. Holman had wanted Anne to wait for 'my Geoff' to walk her home, but uppermost in Anne's mind was the fact that she hadn't seen Elizabeth all day and although both Holmans had tried to persuade her that her eldest daughter would be fine, she would rather be home before fully dark.

So it was that with many an admonition Anne had left the Holman's cottage.

Back under the trees it was much darker than Anne had realized. Pulling the twins to her, she did't want a repeat of earlier, she held a hand each and tried to pretend that she wasn't afraid of the dark.

The conversation from Victoria and Mary revolved solely around the Holmans. Mr. Holman had been given a Godlike status after his trick with the deer and non-stop stories about the creatures of the woods. Mrs. Holman was not far behind after her exploits in the kitchen. Any attempt to engage them otherwise had proved a waste of time. Not that she had tried too hard, it was good that they had managed to forget their father and start to have fun. Part of the healing process, she assumed.

Further along the path Anne could make out a figure crouching in the gloom.

Assuming it to be Geoff Holman, he was after all supposed to be heading back home at any moment, she stopped. She wasn't sure that she was ready to see him yet. She knew that she was attracted to him, which in itself was strange. She had never been one to fall head over heels in love, neither had she ever put too much faith in love at first sight. Nevertheless, after only one meeting she had found herself thinking of him and not just as a friend. Which, again, was strange. She had only just lost her husband.

Steeling herself to the inevitable, she carried on towards the crouching figure. She resolved herself to appear as natural as possible.

"Hi, Geoff." No answer.

The twins halted nervously. Something was wrong.

Peering against the deepening dark she could make out two eyes looking at her. Yellow eyes.

Suddenly afraid, she pushed the twins behind and started to back away.

The eyes moved towards her and she could make out a large, black shape detach itself from the surrounding shadows.

Trying to remain calm she whispered to the twins, "Run back to Mr. and Mrs. Holman's house. Now!" Her whisper had ended up as a shout as she turned and literally pushed them into a run.

She risked a glance back over her shoulder as the thing hit. It was massive. She had fallen face down on the path, but couldn't move. The weight of the creature pressed her onto the hardened mud of the path.

"Run," she screamed, she could think only of the twins. But she needn't have worried, the creature remained upon her. She felt it's hot breath on her neck, she could see one paw next to her face. Grey brindled fur ending in long black claws.

It gave a low growl and she could feel it lower it's head towards her. Dribble from it's open mouth spattered onto her head and neck. Hot.

She fought to rise, to turn over, all to no avail. Although she wasn't aware of it she was screaming hysterically.

She felt the teeth close onto her neck somehow gently as though a lover's kiss. Then she heard the pounding of feet and could see torches bobbing towards her.

Another low growl and it was gone. She felt the weight leave her body.

With a sigh, darkness came crashing in and there was nothing.

*

The first sign Elizabeth had of anything being wrong was a pounding on the door to the cottage. She started from her prone position in front of the fireplace where she had spent the last few hours waiting for her family to return.

The only interruption had been Geoff Holman coming to deliver the wood for the fire. He had lit it, chatted to her for a while and then left. At first she had hated the fact that he had gone, but then, as the night before, she had been mesmerised by the fire. At first just watching the flames feeling an inner peace and then, gradually, she had become more fixed on the flame at the back of the fire. It was darker, somehow, than the others. Dark red as opposed to the yellow, orange flames of the rest of the fire.

She had been snapped rudely from her flame-gazing and looked through the window in the top of the door.

Outside was Geoff, two old people, her sisters, but most of all in Geoff's arms was her mother. A jealous rage overwhelmed her and she snatched the door open.

The old lady rudely pushed her to one side and before she could open her mouth to berate her for it, the twins mobbed her.

"Mum's been attacked," said one.

"A beast, it chased us," cried the other.

Looking down at them, their distress was evident. Both had been crying, and each looked scared half to death.

As she looked back up, the unasked question written across her features, Geoff tenderly carried her mother into the front room.

"What's happened?" she asked .

The old man answered, "Looks like she disturbed a badger or something from what she said, saw something like that run off as we got to her."

Her mother raised her head from where she had been laid on the settee, "No, it was bigger than a badger, it was like a wolf or something."

The old man and Geoff exchanged an unreadable look, if Elizabeth hadn't been watching them she would have missed it.

"No wolves hereabouts," the old man announced. She guessed he was Geoff's father. "Haven't been for hundreds of years - no, what it was was a badger. Big buggers some of them. If you catch 'em when they're out with their young they get protective. Don't usually attack folk, but you never can tell." So saying, it appeared that the matter was cleared up.

Geoff knelt in front of the fire and stoked it, adding more wood which began to flame hungrily. Elizabeth watched him and felt herself stirring with desire, when he discreetly pulled something from his jacket and threw it into the flames. Before she could ask what he was doing, Mrs. Holman bustled in from the kitchen and gave Anne a mug of steaming brew.

"I've made you a cup of something to help you sleep dear. Best thing for you if you've had a bit of a shock."

Elizabeth watched as her mother was nursemaided into drinking the drink. A blanket was produced from somewhere and tucked around her. Her mother's eyes fixed on hers. Something was wrong. That much was obvious. But what? Her mother's eyes held her own briefly then glazed in sleep. Within moments the Holman family stood.

Mrs. Holman turned to her and with strict orders not to disturb her sleeping mother ushered everyone from the room. Taking the twins by the hand she marched them upstairs, leaving her alone with Geoff and his father.

Again, she felt herself forgetting everything else as she looked at Geoff. Her feeling of the last few hours welled up inside, threatening to overwhelm her. Far stronger than before. It took all her strength of will not to throw herself on him there and then.

As if realising, Geoff smiled at her.

Then Mrs. Holman was back. "We'll leave you for now dear, be back in the morning though, see that your mother's OK."

As they all left, Elizabeth ignoring her instructions, went back into the living room. She checked her mother who was deep in sleep.

She curled up in front of the now blazing fire, which had started to give off a faint peculiar smell. Remembering that Geoff had thrown something onto it earlier, she searched to see if she could find out what it was. At the back of the fire was the dark red flame she had seen before.

Unbidden, all her memories of Geoff came flooding back. His face, his body, everything.

Each thought more delicious than the last, she laid her head down and slept, dreaming of Geoff.

As her and her mother lay asleep, the flame at the back of the fire blazed high. Spreading until it engulfed the whole of the fire.

As the carven demon and wolves looked on, mother and daughter slept, bathed in the reflected light. The colour of blood.

*

As before, the man squatted in his hiding place at the edge of the clearing. The light from the living-room window had turned red as he knew it would.

Almost cursing his eagerness earlier that evening with the attack on the mother. But everything had turned out alright. They had all agreed.

Chapter 5

She looked out through a red haze.

Everything was moving along a pace, she would have preferred that the attack on the mother had not occurred so soon, but there would be time to remedy that later. No point in scaring them off before they were tied inextricably to her.

The mother was asleep, she could see the lines of power connecting her, glowing faintly with a reddish tint. That was good. She would require far more attention yet. It was harder working with adults. You had to proceed much more carefully as they were much more likely to notice any changes in their own personality. However, she could taste the woman's emotional turmoil, firstly the death of her husband, and secondly the reawakening of desire with the woodsman.

Her hunger to drink from the welllspring of this woman's innermost feelings was great, but as nothing when compared to the adolescent now curled in front of her. The girl's tangled emotions feeding her, making her strong. Far stronger than the offerings which had sustained her through the centuries. If her so-called acolytes ever realised her ever increasing powers they would be appalled. Even now she was powerful enough to be rid of them. They would keep her as a genie in a bottle. She stretched out her powers, revelling in the new found freedom, and touched upon the sleeping mother.

She could feel the poisons inflicted by the bites of the beast working insidiously through the woman's system. She healed the scratches and abrasions on the back of the neck, not curing the infection, not that, but ridding the woman of any outward signs of the attack. Invading her dreams was more her line, suggestions, once planted, were eagerly consumed by the dreamer. With a dream you could make anybody think anything, but for now it was enough to change her attitudes to the attack. The woman had fallen asleep thinking to leave the next day, torn between the need to remain and heal the hurts of her family and leaving for their protection from the wild beasts of the woods. It was laughable. Laughable and easy to plant the suggestions that everything was fine. Everything pointing to why she should stay. Coupled with the fact that she bore no injuries the woman would see no reason to leave. Quite the opposite, with the changes in her eldest child, there would be every reason to stay.

She turned her attention back to the daughter. Here was a veritable feast of raw emotion. Combined with the normal confusion of an adolescent's emotions was the loss of a father, the lust for the woodsman.

Each feeling multiplying the others a thousandfold. She drank deeply. The girl was almost hers.

Leaving the cottage which had seen her demise, for the first time in centuries, her spirit soared, she visited her acolytes. All deep in sleep except him who kept watch over her cottage.

To each she planted her suggestions, when they woke in the morning each would have the impression that she was still in a weakened state. None would realise her increasing power, not until it was far too late. They had kept her at a subsistence level for far too long. Them and their ancestors through the ages, making the due sacrifices necessary to sustain her, enough so that she grant them special powers, but not so much that she could take matters in hand for herself. Well those days were over. Content as she had been to be kept alive in this manner, biding her time. Let them think for now that she was still bound to the flames as she had been since they had first found her.

Now she was almost free, free to carry on her works. Then they would truly become her acolytes.

Lastly she visited him who held the vigil. He was hers. The only one who truly had the desire to have her back. By his design and his alone these current events had come to pass. To him she gave the vision of what he had to look forward to if he remained faithful to her. She would take him to husband, not to stand as her equal, never that, but above all the others excepting her. The rewards he would receive were legion. Even as she left his mind, now consumed with lust for her, she knew it was coming to pass.

Her return.

*

As Elizabeth woke, dawn was just beginning to creep across the woods outside. Bearing in mind the traumas of the night before, she felt rested. Sitting up she looked into the dying embers of the fire. The now familiar red flame was still dancing, now gleefully it seemed, at the back of the fireplace. She peered closer. Peculiar how the logs there had taken on the aspect of small bones. She gazed at it for a while until they too crumbled to ash along with the rest of the logs. The little red flame clung to the back of the fireplace for a few more moments, and then slowly climbed the chimney, burning the soot in crazed spirals until it left her view.

She rose, thinking to be cramped after her sleep on the floor, but found herself curiously loosened, as if she'd had a thorough massage like at her mother's health club that time.

She looked down at her mother, still fast asleep. Careful not to wake her she stole one of her cigarettes and left to go outside for a crafty smoke. On the porch was a dead sparrow. It looked like the plaything of a deranged cat. It's tiny body covered in blood. Knowing how squeamish her mother could be she picked it up, cradling it in her hands, careful not to damage it's frail body further. Where to put it? If she put it in the dustbin Anne would be sure to see it, scream the house down. Pathetic. That wouldn't do. The fire. Now there was the place, subconciously reminded of the bone-effect of the logs turning to ash moments before, perfect, no remains.

Elizabeth crept back into the living room, stealthily she cast the body onto the fire and covered it with new logs. In an instant the red flame returned, crazily dancing upon the logs which duly ignited. Fire couldn't have gone out properly she thought to herself. A faint peculiar odour pervaded her senses, not that it disgusted her, just an odd smell. She knew it, but could not place where she'd smelt it before.

Returning to the porch, musing about the odour, she lit her cigarette and strolled across the clearing, into the woods.

She wandered aimlessly at first , but as time went on it dawned upon her that she was retracing her steps of the previous morning. She had already passed the tree where she had rested, thinking of her father, and was approaching the clearing where she had first seen Geoff. She realized that this was what she had set off to do, although no conscious decision had been made.

The thrill of excitement at seeing him again made her feel hot inside, with butterflies the size of elephants thundering around her stomach she entered the glade.

He wasn't there.

Disappointment crashed down around her.

He'd said that he was always here or hereabouts. His exact words.

Her earlier good mood was fast dissolving. She had wanted to see him. To talk to him. To prove that she wasn't just a silly schoolgirl. To put her arms around him. To feel his arms around her, his body against hers. She closed her eyes at the thought, lust tearing at her.

She waited, imagining him striding towards her. What he would do. She imagined herself in all manner of situations, with him.

But he wasn't there.

She turned from the glade, the sun peeping over the trees by now, she supposed she should get back.

As she walked back down the path she saw a movement up ahead. Mindful of what had happened the previous night to her mother, she froze.

Hidden by bushes and the pieces of night not yet dispelled by the early morning sun, the movement got closer.

Should she scream? No, the thought was banished immediately. She wasn't going to humiliate herself. Not like her mother had, all over a badger or whatever. What did she expect? This was the countryside. No, she would wait until she could at least see what it was.

Despite her feelings of bravery, they were nothing compared to the initial sense of relief and all the other feelings that hit her when Geoff appeared. His long easy strides carrying him straight to her.

"Good morning," he called out cheerfully. "Hey, are you OK? You look like you've seen a ghost, or at least a badger!" he laughed.

"Yeah, I'm fine. It's just that, well you know after last night, with mother and all..." Damn, she hadn't meant to mention that.

However, the way he put his arm around her shoulders to comfort her made her think that perhaps she was right to mention it.

"Where've you been?" he enquired. Her head pressed close to his chest, she heard it more a a bass rumble than anything else. She clung to him, feeling her passions rise within her, threatening to choke any words that might come out.

"Just for a walk," she replied, her voice made husky by the proximity of this man.

"Yeah, nice enough morning alright."

"Mmm," she nuzzled closer to him, but he didn't seem to notice.

"Were you going home?"

"I was, but I'm not in any hurry," she didn't want him to leave.

"Walk you home, if you want?" he offered.

"OK, but I don't want to stop you from doing anything."

"No, it's OK. I was just about to go there anyway. Make sure everything was alright. You know, see if you wanted anything." Surely he'd just come from there? He looked down at her.

Her pulse raced. Did he mean what she thought he meant? Anything?

He tightened his embrace momentarily then released her. She thought that her knees would buckle. Anything. He reached out a hand and she clasped it. Anything. Her breath thundered in her ears. Just one kiss. She turned her face up to him, her lips parting slightly and it happened.

He lowered his mouth onto hers and kissed her hungrily. At that moment, that glorious moment she would have done anything for him. Her mind soared to the clouds, the passion in his kiss unlocked every emotion in her body, and she felt warm in her abdomen.

All too soon it was over.

"I'm sorry," he apologized.

"No, no please, it was wonderful." She could hardly breathe. Her heart hammered in her breast, her hands sweating freely.

"No, I shouldn't have done that."

He pulled away and tried to release her hand, but she clutched it to her. "Please," she implored him.

"It's too soon." He fell back on 60s movies cliches. "Come on, I'd better take you home."

He held her hand all the way back to the cottage. He stopped a couple of times and smiled down at her, half nervously, half reassuring.

By the time she had gone ten paces down the path, all thoughts of disappointment at the end of their embrace had fled and for the remainder of the journey she gazed up at him with adoration filming her eyes.

*

As they entered the clearing they passed a curiously flattened area concealed by bushes from the cottage. Although Elizabeth saw it and felt a moment's wonder at what had caused it, Geoff's smile, no hint of nervousness now evident, erased it from her mind.

*

Anne had woken shortly after Elizabeth had left. Far from feeling her daughter's sense of ease she woke with an aura of ill. Nothing she could put a finger on immediately, just a pervading sense of wrong. She was stiff from a bad night's sleep on the couch, and there was an awful smell. She had looked around and it seemed as though Elizabeth had lit the fire before leaving. Stupid girl, she thought, today was quite obviously going to be a scorching hot day and she had lit a blazing fire.

It was then that she remembered the night before. Remembered was the wrong word. She had a vague recollection of something happening, but not what.

It was like a dream, almost as if she'd watched a film before going to bed and her subconcious mind had replayed key events over and over whilst she slept. She felt a feeling of wrongness. Knowing that something important had occurred, it was infuriating, fleeting details flicked tantalisingly across her memory, but try as she might, she could pin none of them down.

And there it was, like a bolt of lightning it came to her. Something had attacked her, bitten her on the back of the neck. Some animal. It was almost like a vivid dream.

She raced upstairs to the bathroom, piling her hair on top of her head, she twisted to and fro with her back to the mirror trying to get a good view of her neck.

She couldn't see anything, couldn't feel anything.

The twins appeared sleepily in the doorway.

"Whassup?" said Vicky.

She crouched down in front of her daughters. "Can you see anything on mummy's neck?" she asked.

The twins dutifully peered and probed at the requested area. Nothing.

"Why?" asked Mary, concern etching on her face.

"Oh, it's nothing, I thought... well, I thought that I had scratched it or something." Anne was beginning to wonder about her sanity. Why, if nothing had happened, was she asleep on the couch?

"Bloody girl!" she spat. Where was Elizabeth? She'd know what was going on.

"What've I done?" cried Mary.

"No, not you two," she turned and cuddled the twins. They must think I'm barmy. "I meant Lizzie, she's gone out again."

The twins sobbing subsided somewhat. "I'm behaving like a bear with a sore head," Anne admonished herself. "Come on," she said in a vain attempt to cheer them up, "Who's for breakfast?"

They looked at her in wonder, in the space of a couple of minutes they had watched her go through a whole cavalcade of emotions. Giving each other a knowing look, they turned to her and nodded.

"Great, they do think I'm crazy."

At that moment there was a knock at the door.

"Right, go and sit down in the living room, I'll see who that is and then get you some grub, OK?"

Again, they nodded dumbly. Anything to keep the peace thought Anne.

She ushered them to the top of the stairs and then patting her hair in an ineffectual attempt to make it look like she hadn't just woken, ran to answer the door.

It was Mrs. Holman.

"My goodness dear, you shouldn't be out of bed, not after what you've been through."

Ah ha, answers. "I'm terribly sorry, Mrs. Holman, but I can't seem to think straight this morning, what exactly did happen?"

"Dear, you had quite a nasty shock, came running as soon as you screamed. Don't you remember? A badger jumped out on you, gave you quite a fright." With one arm around her shoulders, Mrs. Holman steered her into the living room.

"Mum, can we have some breakfast?" the twins sang in unison.

Mrs. Holman shot her a look as if to say that she couldn't look after her own children. "Don't you upset yourself dear, I'll sort them out, you just rest up there." So saying, she pushed Anne down onto the couch and bustled off in the direction of the kitchen.

The twins sat in front of that awful fireplace, knowing that their breakfast was coming, they were now oblivious to Anne's presence.

God, was she the only one who could smell? That disgusting odour whilst not getting any worse had certainly not got any better. Mrs. Holman bustled back into view. "Have you eaten yet dear?" Anne shook her head, she was about to say that she wasn't hungry, but Mrs. Holman had already gone, tutting under her breath.

"Good start to the day," she thought to herself. Leaning back into the couch she closed her eyes and tried to recall the events of the previous night. Still nothing. If she had been attacked, how could she not remember it? Oh, she could remember something happening, but no details. She was getting a headache.

She turned and looked out of the window. Coming across the glade was Elizabeth, holding hands with Geoff Holman, sharing a look that spoke volumes. Jealousy rose within her, engulfing her totally, driving out all else. She could feel herself begin to shake. Behind the jealousy came a towering rage. How dare the girl go around like that? Flirting with Geoff, what a slut!

Her head was pounding fit to burst. Unable to see past her emotions she stood and stumbled towards the door, her face contorted with anger.

Framed in the doorway, Mrs. Holman stood with a plate in either hand, her face a mask of horror at the vision before her.

Quickly controlling her features, Mrs. Holman stepped in front of Anne.

"My dear, whatever can be the matter?" She asked, putting the plates down.

Anne tried to reply, her anger wouldn't let any words come out, her utterance a croak.

Speaking softly to her, Mrs. Holman tried to guide her to the stairs. Shaking herself free, Anne stormed down the hall to the front door. Yanking it open she strode onto the porch, her eyes fairly blazing with fury.

And then Geoff was there. A smile, a greeting, a concerned touch on her arm. The anger had gone, replaced by a desire for this man. She must have him. Elizabeth joined them, her worried expression obviously designed to mislead, the slut! Anne felt every muscle in her body ache to hit her daughter, her hands opening and closing reflexively.

Geoff stepped in between them.

"Mother?" called Elizabeth.

"Come on let's get you to bed," Mrs. Holman ventured behind her.

"Yes, you've had a nasty shock, Anne. Come on, I'll help."

Geoff was going to help her to bed! It was wonderful.

Putting an arm around her waist, Geoff encouraged her to step towards the stairs, following the lead set by his mother.

Anne felt drunk at his touch, she leaned into him and let him propel her up the stairs to her room.

Once there, Mrs. Holman was already busily turning down the sheets. "You go son, I'll help Mrs. Masterson to undress."

Anne felt him go, felt it to the very core of her being. It was as if a part of her had left with him. She stood stock still, letting Mrs. Holman undress her. All the time, Mrs. Holman was talking, comments like "What do you expect? No breakfast after a shock like that," and "You shouldn't be up and about, you're too unwell," came through her fogged mind, but didn't penetrate. Her mind was full of Geoff.

Mrs. Holman put her to bed, admonishing her not to move until she was better. A promise of food after she had slept a little and she was gone.

Not that Anne noticed. Even as she lay thinking of him, her headache returned with a vengeance.

She slept.

*

Outside the door Geoff's mother whirled on him angrily.

"What on earth do you think you are doing?" she spat, her matronly personality replaced by one that dripped venom.

"It's all under control, mother," he replied calmly. "You do what you do, but don't interfere with me," he warned. "You try to interfere again and it'll be the worse for you!"

"How dare you," her voice, whilst still barely above a whisper, rasped in his ears. "Wait until I tell your father, then there'll be a reckoning!"

"Ha, you think you know it all, don't you? You don't know the half," he scorned her.

"Just wait, your father'll have something to say about this!"

"Like I care!" Geoff started down the stairs, and this was hissed over his shoulder as if to end the argument.

But Mrs Holman wouldn't let it lie at that, she charged down the stairs after him and finally caught up with him outside in the clearing. Grabbing his arm she spun him around.

"You listen to me boy. You're going to ruin everything we've got, She's going to get too strong. What'll happen then? Have you thought about that?"

"Maybe that's what I want." Geoff turned to leave again.

"No! You can't. Think Geoff, think" Mrs Holman cried.

"Mother, all I'm doing is following my instructions. Like I'm supposed to. Woo the girl, flirt with the mother, play them off one against the other. That's what I was told, that's what I've done. I suggest that you do the same."

"But Geoff, we'll lose everything. She'll return, what'll we do then?"

"This is what we've been working for. This is what we all planned."

"But it's too soon, what if she decides she doesn't need us any more? What then?"

"Just get on with it mother." Geoff pulled away and disappeared into the woods.

Mrs. Holman looked as if she would follow him and say more, but something about the way her son looked stopped her in her tracks. Quickly reconsidering, she merely huffed and called after him, "I'm going to get the girls something to eat, we'll finish this later." So saying, she turned and walked back into the house.

Unbeknownst to both of them, Elizabeth closed her bedroom door, she hadn't heard the full argument, not much in fact from when they went down the stairs. She wondered what it was that Geoff had done to infuriate his mother so. But the old bag annoyed her so it was hardly surprising that Geoff would get exasperated now and again. It wasn't as if Mrs Holman was a horrible woman really, but she was always around, fussing. One of the reasons that they had come all the way out here was to get away from all the do-gooders and now they were being smothered by the queen of do-good. Always so right, always so nice. Always there! That was the problem. Serve her right if Geoff left her.

Now there was a thought.

Chapter 6

Whilst her mother slept upstairs, Elizabeth hunkered down in front of the fire and tried to make sense of the last couple of days. She supposed that she could put her mother's actions of earlier down to some sort of reaction to shock, but it didn't quite ring true.

With the twins gone – they had left with Mrs. Holman to go through the woods with her husband - she had ample opportunity to think things through.

The fact of the matter was that she couldn't. Resigning herself to never understanding exactly what had occurred, she rose, stealing another of her mother's cigarettes she went outside into the glade and smoked.

She had already put Mrs. Holman's behaviour down to some sort of mother/son argument and she wouldn't have been half surprised to find out that it was about her. She stretched up on to her tiptoes and revelled in the thought.

*

Putting her arms behind her head, Elizabeth stretched out on her bed. All the activities of the last few weeks were slowly catching up with her and she felt unreasonably tired, which was making it more difficult to think straight.

Rolling onto her stomach she began to question her reaction to Geoff's advances. Although she supposed advances was too strong a word. She had to face facts, she had been desperate for him to kiss her since the first meeting, she'd almost contrived to get him alone so that he could 'advance' on her.

She pushed her face into her pillow and squirmed, half embarassed, half delighted. If only he'd advanced a little further, she thought to herself.

And then stopped.

One minute she was finding it difficult to think rationally about monumentous moments in her recent past, the death of her father, the peculiar attack on her mother and in the next breath she was becoming sexually charged by the indecent thoughts of a kiss in the woods. What the hell was happening to her?

Whilst not the brightest girl in her class, she certainly wasn't stupid, quite the reverse. She had always prided herself on her ability to logically analyse most things. It might take her a bit longer than some to fathom things out, but she always got there in the end.

The longer Elizabeth thought about it, the more convinced she became that something wasn't quite right.

It was with this thought that she finally dozed off.

She was woken by a knocking at the door. After a second's disorientation she realised she'd slept most of the afternoon through. Looking out of her bedroom window the sun was beginning to dip beneath the tops of the surrounding trees.

The knocking was repeated and she jumped up from her bed and ran downstairs to answer it, to be confronted by Mrs. Holman and the twins.

"Er, hi. Come in," she offered.

"Did I wake you my dear?" asked Mrs. Holman with a knowing look.

"Yeah, I must've been tireder than I realised. Just nodded off," Elizabeth explained.

"Well, I've just brought these two home, I was going to get them some tea and check on your mother, of course. Can I get you anything?"

Elizabeth knew that the old lady was just trying to be helpful, but she was only succeeding in winding her up.

A noise from upstairs caused all four of them to look up the stairs. At the top Anne stood weakly holding the end of the bannister, as if to prevent herself from falling. Her gown, hastily adorned, hung loosely from her shoulders, gaping widely at the front. Her skin was soaked with sweat, her hair plastered to her head. Wide eyes stared unseeing from her face which fairly shone, it was so red.

Elizabeth gasped and broke the silence, the inactivity was broken by Mrs. Holman who grabbed Elizabeth's arm. Elizabeth turned to look, the question evident in her eyes. What was going on? She was prevented from asking by the horror etched into Mrs. Holman's features.

"She's too strong," whispered Mrs. Holman.

"What?"

Mrs. Holman visibly wilted, sagging back against the door. "Too strong. Something's wrong."

"What's going on, what's wrong with her?"

Steeling herself, Mrs. Holman started up the stairs. Never taking her eyes from Anne she told Elizabeth "Take the girls out of here. Now!"

Elizabeth caught hold of her sisters, who had witnessed the whole incident and propelled them into the living room. The girls instantly dashed to the fireplace and sat down in front of it. Holding hands and looking directly into each others' eyes, they sat quietly. Too quietly.

"Are you two alright?" she enquired.

They both nodded, but said nothing.

Elizabeth sat down by the window and looked out into the gathering gloom as dusk stole across the glade. She could hear the twins behind her as they stoked the fire, the warmth from the blaze pushing away the chill of early evening. As she continued to stare outside, her worry for her mother was dispelled momentarily by the clouds gathering on the horizon. It looked stormy. "Great," she thought to herself.

She was brought out of her reverie by that peculiar smell. Sniffing, she turned to see the twins still messing about with the fire.

"Come away from there, before you hurt yourselves," she said exasperated. "The last thing we need now is you two setting fire to each other. Bloody kids!"

"What've you put on there?" she stood and moved between the twins and the fireplace. Was it her imagination, or was that a feather? Whatever, the flames devoured the evidence in that instant.

"What was it?" she shouted.

The twins shared another look and then turned innocent smiles upon her.

"You little bastards, you've killed something haven't you?" she screamed at the last.

"Quiet now!" Mrs. Holman's voice cracked like a whip, "Your mother's sleeping."

The twins ignored her and continued to look into the fire.

"Would you like something to eat?"

"No." Elizabeth had to bite her tongue to hold back the torrent of abuse that threatened to flood out. She ran from the room, torn between her concern for her mother and her desire to be alone. She chose the latter and fled into the woods.

*

Anne thrashed in her bed and sat bolt upright. She looked around her room through a red haze. It was the same room, but everything was different. Vastly different. The decor, the furniture. Everything. She walked to the window and realized she couldn't remember standing. Turning back to look at the room she was surprised to see the bed gone, replaced by a low, straw stuffed pallet. Her first impression was weird, but this was slowly changed to a feeling of rightness. This was how it should look.

She looked back out of the window, no matter how hard she tried she couldn't pierce the gloom, couldn't see the glade, the surrounding trees. But she knew they would be there. The sky was storm tossed, the clouds black, blacker than pitch.

She didn't know how long she had stood there listening to the call, but it slowly impinged itself on her conciousness.

She turned and walked to the door following the call. It wasn't voiced, she couldn't hear it, but it was there, in her mind.

She slowly stepped down the stairs. Stopping to consider the changes. All around, though she knew she was in the same cottage, she couldn't match any of her surroundings with her memory.

The call led her into the room with the fireplace, as she knew it must, and she halted in front of it.

"KNEEL."

It wasn't a subject for discussion, she must do exactly as commanded. She knelt and pressed her head to the hearth.

The fire blazed and she could hear tortured screams in the background, people, animals, birds, a cacophony of noise.

The voice pushed them away. "IGNORE THEM!" The screams faded.

Anne raised her head from the hearth and stared into the flames. At the rear of the fire one flame, darker than the others, "almost red," she thought, danced crazily. As she watched it steadied and then grew. Larger and larger until it engulfed the whole fire. One sheet of blood red flame. Images flicked through the flame, some she recognised, others she did not. Alongside pictures of her daughters, the twins, feeding the fire, Elizabeth kissing Geoff in the woods, were images she could only assume were from ages past. A young woman consumed by fire, a mob, their faces ugly with hatred in this very room. Suffused with countless pictures of many people worshipping in front of the fire. She saw Mr. and Mrs. Holman copulating in front of the fireplace, their bodies covered in blood, though there was no discernable wound. They were a lot younger, but it was obviously them. Then they were presenting a new-born baby to the fireplace, again it was covered in blood. "Geoff?" she asked herself. But the voice answered "YES."

The images came and went as countless deeds played out in front of the fire were replayed for her now. She was transfixed.

Then they were gone.

A darkness gathered behind the flame. The shadow became a form. A human form. As it became more solid it advanced, passing through the flame. It was the young woman, she had first seen in the flame. The beautiful lady who had burned in the fire.

"DO YOU KNOW ME?"

"Yes." Anne spoke aloud, shock spasmed her entire body as the entity entered into her. She couldn't explain or understand what had happened, she just knew that the beautiful woman had somehow passed into her. She could feel her. Feel her needs, her desires. It was like an electric shock. Anne's stomach tingled, her hair flew around her head, she felt herself becoming aroused. Then it was gone.

She opened her eyes and was surprised to find that she was crying. Her shoulders shook as great sobs rose within her. Tears streaming down her face. She wanted her back, back inside her. It was like a drug, she had just experienced the most tremendous high, now she wanted it again and again and again, and she would do anything to get it.

"I CAN GIVE YOU EVERYTHING."

"I want you back," Anne cried. Her hands clasped before her. She was begging, but didn't care.

"AID ME AND YOU CAN."

"What must I do? Just say and I'll do it."

She felt the presence enter her again and trembled as passion waved through her body, greater than the touch of any man. Her head arched back and she howled with pleasure. Slowly, images came again. But these were subtly different, she understood. These were not the past. These were instructions.

Anne nodded. "Yes, command me, I am yours," she pledged.

"SLOWLY. FIRST YOU MUST BE MINE."

Anne laid back giving herself over completely to the woman. Pleasure oozed from every pore as she fell into blackness.

*

Anne woke. It was full dark now. She had the vaguest memories of the last few days, but uppermost in her mind were the tasks she had been set.

She dressed quickly and went downstairs. Mrs. Holman was asleep on the settee. She left her there.

The twins were sat in vigil in front of the fireplace. As she entered the lounge the twins stood and all three embraced. They knew, she thought.

All three knelt in front of the fire and bathed in the glory of the blood red flame.

Chapter 7

Elizabeth had run out into the gathering gloom, rather than cross the glade as she had always done in the past, she had chosen to run into the woods behind the house. For no other reason than it was away from everybody, and it took her further from the Holmans cottage with every step.

She couldn't face anyone in her current mood, the twins were up to something, but she couldn't fathom what. It seemed as though they had burned some bird on the fire, but why would they? It made no sense at all, neither of the girls had ever shown a cruel streak in the past. Quite the reverse, they were both exceptionally squeamish and were both forever 'rescuing' injured creatures to nurse back to health. She must be mistaken, but they had both been acting so oddly recently. Perhaps they all had. Nobody had coped well with the death of their father, so should she forget what she had seen and resolve to be more understanding? She just didn't know. It was all out of her scope, it was a psychiatrist's field day.

Her mother as well. Christ, there was a fruitcake in the making. Pretty much as soon as they had arrived she had gone off the rails. Shouting and screaming at all and sundry. Then that attack, wouldn't be surprised if she'd made all that up. In a second she was contrite. Of course she hadn't. That something had happened was never in question. But it was all so strange, and her mother flirting with Geoff. Now that was pathetic, she was twice his age, how could she forget her husband so readily?

Elizabeth knew she was being unfair, but she had hit a theme with her thoughts and would lash out at anyone, especially where Geoff was concerned.

Without thinking she pulled a cigarette from her pocket and lit it. The first drag, after all her musings, left her light-headed, but she pulled at it again and again. Smoking it right down to the stub, never mind the public health warnings listed on the packet. Without realising what she was doing she crushed the butt into the springy moss underfoot and automatically lit another.

She didn't want to think about Geoff, but as always he pushed all other thoughts away. With him in her mind she plunged deeper into the woods. In this region there was no path as such, but she could find a way through most of the brambles and nettles which proliferated under the trees, sometimes more by luck than judgement as she sucked another finger which had caught on a thorn. This suited her mood, her twisting through the woods a reflection of her twisting thought processes. Would it always be that way with Geoff? She sighed and came to the conclusion that it probably always would. He wouldn't do what she wanted she thought bitterly to herself. She pulled at her jumper which had snagged on a bramble. Swearing under her breath she freed herself and continued her wayward journey. Muttering to herself, the whole world seemed against her at this moment she thought as she stumped along as if trying to beat the earth with every footstep.

Then it started to rain.

Not a light drizzle, no bloody chance, massive drops, which came crashing through the tree canopy. Within seconds her hair was plastered to her face, no amount of scraping at it would keep it from her eyes for more than a couple of seconds. Not that it mattered because she couldn't see the back of her hand in front of her face. She looked around. It was black, whereas a couple of minutes before it was gloomy, she could make out the trees around her as blacker pieces of the surrounding shadow. Now she couldn't even do that. With no obvious path before or behind her she had no idea where she was, let alone which direction the cottage lay in. The reality came crashing in. She was lost. She began to shiver, her jumper, her trousers, Christ, even her underwear was soaked.

With a crash of thunder which left her senses reeling it was so loud, a sheet of lightning lit up the sky above the trees. Down in the gloom it was more of a patchy flash of white brilliance which left a purplish after-image of her immediate surroundings.

She was truly terrified, watching these storms on the telly or from a cosy fireside was one thing, but to be left to the mercy of these primordial elements left Elizabeth gasping for breath. She could feel the panic choking her.

Suddenly, she had a warm feeling. Just a thought of her father. His hand reaching out to grasp hers. "Don't worry," the thought was unbidden, but she took solace. She wasn't alone and never would be. She would always have her father. Fortified by this, she waited for the next lightning strike. It came dazzling in it's intensity, again she held the after-image. A great tree bole was straight ahead of her. She thought nothing of the danger only of shelter from the rain. She wasn't frightened.

Taking the first step she knew that she only need to stay on course. The second step was even easier and the third easier than that. The fourth step was never finished as she stepped off into nothingness. She fell forward and hit the ground hard, putting her hands out to grab roots of plants or anything which would slow her slide, her hands were torn and bleeding by the time she hit the bottom of the defile she had crashed into. She lay dazed and confused, battered and bruised.

It was a few minutes before she tried to sit up. "Nothing broken," she thought, but everything hurt nonetheless. She gave up and curled into a tight ball sobbing uncontrollably. Shivering, partly with the cold, but mostly with shock. With her knees pulled in hard to her chest, she lay and cursed everybody and everything that had ever led to her being here. Her eyes shut tight against the world, she flinched with every thunderbolt.

And still it rained.

*

A hand upon her shoulder startled her from her misery.

"Are you OK?"

Elizabeth opened her eyes slowly, but a bright light made her squeeze them shut again…

"Sorry." There was a click and then she opened them again. It was Geoff.

"Are you OK?" he asked again, his voice now had a frantic quality which she hadn't noticed before.

"Yes… yes, I think so," she trembled.

"We've got to get you out of those wet clothes and dry. You're going to catch pneumonia if you stay like this. What are you doing out here anyway?"

The torch clicked back on and Geoff was struggling out of his coat. "Here, put this on, it'll help to keep the rain off, stop you from getting wetter."

He pulled her to her feet and threaded her arms into the coat sleeves.

She looked at him, his shirt until now dry had started to get darker where the raindrops landed.

"But you'll get wet."

"You let me worry about me. Can you walk? Right let's get you warmed up then," he announced in response to her dumb nod.

Geoff guided her along the defile, through the undergrowth, where it opened onto a track, easy to see in the torch light.

Thunder crashed around them and Elizabeth flinched, pulling Geoff to her. He put his arm around her. "Hey, it's OK. How long have you been out there? And why were you out in all of this?"

"I just needed to get out. Get away from everyone for a while. It got too dark to see and I fell. I couldn't find a path."

"Well, it's a good job I was out and about, you could have been there for ages."

"How did you know where I was?"

"Eh?"

"Well, I wasn't on the path or anything, so how did you find me?"

"You should just be glad I did. Come on, let's get you dried off."

This effectively cut off any further conversation. Geoff walked ahead. The path was made slick by the rain which if anything was coming down even harder. Elizabeth slithered rather than walked behind him. Her eyes concentrating on the small pool of torchlight, when they were not blinded by the lightning strikes which were increasing in regularity. After slipping over for the third time she wailed plaintively, "How much further?"

Geoff stopped and looked around. His eyes seemed almost feral in the light. Like a light shone from within. Elizabeth recoiled.

The moment passed and Geoff turned to face forwards again.

"I'll take you to our place, it's nearer."

"Good. I'm not really in the mood to see the family right now."

"Come on then."

She stumbled after him for another age, or so it seemed. Though it was probably only about half an hour.

It was so dark that she did't realise they had arrived until she started up the steps to the cottage.

"Nobody else home," Geoff announced.

"Mmm," Elizabeth agreed sleepily. She hadn't realised how tired she was.

"Come on, I'll run you a bath." Elizabeth stood still while Geoff took his coat off her. Slightly dazed she allowed herself to be lead into the living-room, where Geoff stoked the old Raeburn. "You get out of those wet things and I'll get you some towels. Come on, this is not time for false modesty, if you stand there you'll catch a chill." So saying, he left her.

Elizabeth stripped down to her underwear and a T-shirt which, though soaked through, she wasn't prepared to prance about in the nude. Geoff came back in, his arms full of towels. "I've started the bath for you." If he noticed that she hadn't undressed fully, he didn't say anything, but Elizabeth thought he looked amused. She wrapped a towel around herself and started rubbing to get her circulation going again. She looked over to Geoff and to her surprise he was just putting a gown on, his clothes a cumpled heap on the floor. Why hadn't she looked a moment earlier?

"Come on, get in the bath and I'll bring you something to drink." He led her by the hand to the bathroom, as he opened the door great gouts of steam escaped. "Back in a minute." He left her. She turned and shut the door, but there was no lock.

"Oh, well," she thought to herself. She let the towel fall to the ground and finished undressing, stepping gingerly into the piping hot water. She sat and let out a sigh of relief. She lay back and shut her eyes letting the water ease away her chill, which felt as though it had penetrated through to her very bones. Eyes still closed, she slid deeper until her head dipped below the surface of the water. This was divine. She lay like that for as long as possible and then pushed herself back up to lay with her head resting on the back of the bath. Finally warm, she massaged her muscles, getting all the aches out.

"Here you are."

She leapt like a startled rabbit, her heart in her mouth.

Reaching around she grabbed a flannel and attempted to cover herself.

Geoff stood over the bath and handed her a steaming mug.

"Thanks," she stammered. Looking up at him, he had a strange look in his eyes.

"Feel a bit better?"

She felt awful, still squirming in embarassment, she tried to cover it by sipping the drink. It raced down her throat like fire. She coughed, her throat raw. "What is it?," she asked, making a face.

"Hot toddy. Best thing for you. Warm you up from the inside." He laughed.

"Would you just leave me for a moment while I finish my bath?"

After all her daydreaming of exactly such a situation the reality left a lot to be desired. Geoff standing there in his bathrobe grinning at her. It wasn't going the way she had imagined.

"Of course," he replied, making her feel churlish, he had after all just probably saved her life. Which again raised the question.

"How did you know where I was?"

He turned from the door and was about to answer when his head shot up. His grin gone, he put his head on one side as if listening. After standing like that for a moment, she could hear him murmuring "No, it can't be," over and over. As if to emphasize his momentary inactivity, he suddenly became animated.

"Stay here!" he ordered. His voice was gruff, the words mangled somehow.

"Where are you going?" Any thoughts of prudishness gone, Elizabeth tried to stand.

"Stay here." He was gone.

Elizabeth stood, feeling foolish she grabbed a fresh towel from the rail and wrapped it round herself. She would try to recover whatever dignity she had left. She heard the door go downstairs, following the noise she went to the door and opened it. There was no sign of Geoff, but on the ground at her feet showing faintly in the gloom, was his bath robe.

Chapter 8

As the flames blazed, Anne added some more logs and the twins placed their latest collection of animals. As they did so, the red flame came forward to consume their offering. The blood red flame was evident constantly and had grown in size, hungrily burning every sacrifice as if feeding itself. As the last vestiges of the offerings were accepted and burned the flame again spread to form a sheet of blood red fire, roaring now that the other flames were subdued. The room was bathed in the light.

Anne and the twins hugged before the flame and turned to look at the room. Mrs. Holman still lay asleep on the settee.

Victoria shared a glance with her twin, passing their silent communication, with a nod she rose and strode purposefully to the recumbent form of Mrs. Holman. Raising her hand high above her head she brought it down across Mrs. Holman's face in a full open-handed slap. The crack of the blow sounded sharp in the silence. Mrs. Holman came to, her eyes wide open in shock and disbelief. She struggled to a seating position and rubbed her cheek, her eyes tearing from the sting. Recognition dawned on her as Victoria's hand was raised to repeat the blow. Her upraised hand was caught in a tight painful grip as Mrs. Holman tried to make sense of what had happened.

"You frightful child," she spat venomously. She pulled her own hand back to deliver a punishing slap, but froze as she saw what was going on behind Victoria.

Anne and Mary rose from their kneeling positions in front of the fireplace and the blood red flame rose with them. Their features unreadable as they advanced towards the settee. The deep red light behind them left them as shadows.

"It's over Mrs. Holman, let my daughter go."

"What? This little bitch just hit me. If you think that I'm going to forget about that you've got another think coming. I'll see to it that you all pay." She turned to stare at Victoria and again pulled her hand back. Before she could finish her blow, however, her head snapped back from the punch that Mary delivered. Her amazement was obvious. Her hand fell and she released Victoria. Her eyes wide, her mouth opening and closing, but she couldn't articulate any words.

Victoria and Mary glanced back to their mother who merely nodded her affirmation. This unleashed a torrent of blows from the twins whose strength was far above that of their size. Mrs. Holman covered her head and sobbed uncontrollably as kicks were added to the punches as she fell from the settee.

Crawling on her stomach she tried to escape, but Victoria and Mary flew on her in a rage, as if they were possessed. The attack was made sinister by their silence, the only sounds those of the blows and Mrs. Holman's moans.

All at once the door to the living room opened and Mr. Holman raced in. "What the blazes?" He pulled Victoria off of his wife who looked up, her face puffed and swollen. Before he could say anything else, Mary leapt up and drove her fingers at his eyes, his head recoiled backwards and he let drop her twin.

The girls diverted their attention to the old man and left Mrs. Holman a huddled shape on the floor. Although not a weak man, he was no match for the twins with their almost superhuman strength. Forced to his knees he could only try to defend himself and raised his arms protectively over his face.

As the onslaught continued Anne began speaking. It was not her normal voice. It was deeper, richer. It was Her voice.

"You have betrayed me. I, who gave you everything. You have knowingly kept me starved of energy. Kept me weak where I should have been strong. If not for these lovely girls, I would have remained so. How long did you think you could keep me so? How long did you think this would go unnoticed? I would have rewarded you for your devotion, but you have betrayed me."

The voice rose in pitch until at the last it became a scream. Hands raised claw-like above her head, her hair tossed wildly by an unfelt wind. Her image black against the back-drop of the fire. Her damning litany continued.

Mr. Holman fell to the floor with a thud. Mrs. Holman, left alone, had dragged herself to the fireplace. Reaching out for anything to strike back with, her hand fell upon the poker. Gripping it tightly in one hand she raised it to strike at Anne. The twins turned their attention upon her, but it was too late. Before the blow could fall, however, a bolt of flame lanced from the fire and shot the length of the poker to her hand. Screaming in agony, Mrs. Holman tried to drop it, but the flame had taken hold.

Without sparing her a glance, Anne continued.

"These people are now my acolytes. They shall prepare the way for my return. To them, I shall give my love, and my gifts in return for their adoration. You are as nothing. NOTHING. You will agree to serve me by aiding them, give them your all, or I will destroy you, as though you had never been."

The flame leapt back into the fire and Mrs. Holman cried with relief. The poker clattered noisily to the floor. Before unconciousness took her, she gazed up through hate-filled eyes, knowing that she had lost.

By the door, Mr. Holman was in no better shape. Curled in a foetal position he had blacked out under the beating from the twins. But that was no escape from Her. Leaving Anne, she floated into his subconcious and continued his torture. The only outward signs were his continued low moans as his body flinched in response to his mind's pain.

Holding hands with her daughters, Anne approached the fireplace. Kicking the body of Mrs. Holman to one side, they all knelt and pressed their foreheads on the floor in homage. Anne had completed the first of the tasks that she had been set. The Holmans had never been any better than adequate servants of the flame. Always more interested with what they would receive from Her. Not wanting Her return as that would presage an end to their way of life. Selfish goodfornothings had had their comeuppance. The thrill of it sent shivers down the spines of all three.

*

Geoff's response was immediate. Whenever danger threatened or whenever she required, Her gift to him manifested itself. As he took off across the glade to Her cottage, his form changed. Mid-stride, he fell to all fours. His mouth unable to speak properly to Elizabeth moments before lengthened into a snout, his tongue which had mangled his words lolled out to the side. As his hands hit the earth they split and curled back on themselves becoming paws. Without stopping his transformation became complete as his spine extended into the tail and his whole body bristled with fur. The change from man into wolf took less than a second. The speed of his passing across the glade, even less, as he raced towards the danger.

Even as he tore through the woods his witch-keen senses told him that something was wrong in the cottage. He couldn't feel his mother or father as he knew he should. Their presence was faint, whereas he could normally feel them from miles away. The power usually so subdued was drawing him like a lode-stone to the cottage.

As he leaped across the clearing and through the door, the sense of wrongness hit him. But he could not slow.

As a wolf he crashed into the living-room. The still forms of his parents took his mind for a mere moment when the source of his torment became apparent. The woman in front of the fire had been with Her! She had lain with this bitch, whilst he had been out doing his bidding. Jealousy engulfed him and he sprang at the woman knelt in front of the fire.

He landed atop the kneeling form and all three humans screamed. He wasn't concerned with the two children. Only the woman. The woman who had, behind his back, taken and empowered Her. He was to be Hers. No-one else. In his rage he was without thought. Tearing with his mouth at the offending woman, his hands scratching down her back.

Hands.

The thought pushed aside his rage for a moment. Hands, where were his paws? Pausing briefly he searched his arms. His all too human arms. He fell back and as he did so the children lit into him. His shock was so great that he didn't register until he felt the first rib crack. He had changed back into a man.

He looked up, the emotional pain too great for him to feel the physical blows. It was as though it was happening to someone else.

"Why?" he screamed. His tears streaming down his face. "Why? With this woman!" His plaintive questions were addressed to the fire, but Anne answered him.

"I choose who I will go with and who not. You were to be mine, but in your mind you have betrayed me. The girl. I have felt your lustful thoughts. You and that girl. How long were you going to go on thinking that way before you acted. You have been kept for me, I will not share you with anyone else."

Anger flared up in his breast, "I will not share you." So saying, he flew at Anne, his naked body covered in welts and bruises, but he felt none of them. His rage pushed them all to one side.

Anne's hand flashed up and caught him by the throat, holding him up and then flinging him across the room. He landed awkwardly and heard, rather than felt, his ankle snap.

"Where is she?"

Geoff tried to stand, but the pain of his injuries came upon him, he gasped and fell to the floor.

"Where is she?" The voice that was not Anne's tore from her throat. "She is to be the vessel of my return. I have chosen her. Where is she?"

"We shall help you to find her," chorused the twins. So saying, the three of them left the room, the red flame flickered in the fire. It's glow lighting the devastation.

They passed Geoff without a thought. With his powers gone he was no match for them. They were the new servants. They would bring her back. They only needed one thing. Elizabeth.

*

Elizabeth had wandered around the Holman's cottage, still wrapped in a towel. Outside the rain was sheeting down and she again felt cold. In the kitchen she found the bottle of whisky which had been used to make the hot toddy. Unscrewing the cap she took a swig from the bottle and gasped as a shiver took her. "Christ," she thought, that was rough. However, the fridge contained a bottle of lemonade and finding a glass she mixed the two making it far more palatable.

Taking the glass and bottles upstairs, she looked for Geoff's room. Her own clothes were still soaked and she didn't want to be found by Mr. and Mrs. Holman wearing just a towel!

She opened one door and assuming it to belong to his parents shut it again quickly. Further down the hall, another door was open and a quick look inside revealed this to be the one she was after.

She entered and sat upon the bed. Laying back, her mind wandered to what could have happened earlier in the bathroom. She quickly banished the intruding memories of her panic that he would do anything. In her fantasy she was much more self-assured. He was far more forward and the end result was more delicious than reality had allowed. Her mind, choosing it's own path, had her body squirming on his bed.

What was she thinking of?

He had run off into the night with barely a word! Leaving his gown! Had he been naked underneath? She didn't want to pursue that line of thought. Well, she did.

Sitting up she scanned the room, next to an old-fashioned wardrobe stood an equally old-fashioned chest of drawers. Finishing her drink she crossed the room and opened the wardrobe. In it hung all Geoff's clothes, shirts, jackets, jeans. All neatly pressed and smelling fresh, the smell reminded her faintly of him and she was nearly overcome again.

Pouring another drink she chose a shirt, a thick padded checked shirt, and a pair of worn jeans. The chest of drawers provided a thick pair of socks and a T-shirt, but try as she might, she could find no underwear.

"Mmmm..." she thought, "interesting."

Dressing quickly, or as quickly as she could, her hands had become... well, useless, she fumbled the shirt buttons, fell onto the bed when she tried to put on the socks and when she finally buttoned on the jeans they slipped down and fell in a pool round her ankles. Sitting back down on the bed, she collapsed in a fit of giggles. Reaching for her glass she found it empty. She grabbed for the whisky bottle, twice, the first time she missed it, and poured the remainder of the bottle into her glass, topping it up with lemonade. Taking a large swig she fell towards the wardrobe and rummaging through, managed to find a belt, which was also far too large. Muttering to herself she finally found some string which after much fumbling and swearing finally held the trousers up. Turning them up so she could see her feet, she staggered back to the bathroom. Picking up her own clothes left her slumped against the side of the bath wondering what on earth was wrong with her. She pulled on her sodden trainers and as if that supreme effort was the last straw, she turned and vomited noisily into the toilet.

It was some time before she could lean back again.

She felt rough, not quite so disorientated, but delicate. And her head was beginning to thump.

As she stood, she began to wonder whether she had taken a chill whilst caught out in the rainstorm. She made it back into Geoff's room, her mouth dry and foul tasting. She picked up her glass. Empty. The whisky bottle on the bed. Empty. Half the lemonade remained though and she drank thirstily.

Grabbing a waterproof jacket from the wardrobe which engulfed her when she put it on, she went downstairs and out of the door.

Her mind was fuzzy and she tried to think of where Geoff had gone. He had gone without saying anything really. No, that wasn't quite true, he had told her to wait. But for how long? In fact, how long had he been gone? Was she supposed to wait for Mr. and Mrs. Holman to come back? Not bloody likely.

She looked off into the dark, she wasn't even sure which way to go to get back to her own cottage. Walking out into the clearing, she pulled up the hood of the jacket. The rain was hammering down now. Picking one of the paths, she set off.

*

Anne and the twins walked across the clearing towards the Holman's cottage. Ignoring the discarded robe in the doorway, they entered. Just as they had not noticed the driving rain outside, they did not notice that they had ceased to get wet inside. The weather was as nothing to them. They had one thing and one thing only to consume them. Elizabeth.

As Anne walked into the living room, the twins raced upstairs. Anne stood still for a moment, her arms outstretched. She could feel that Elizabeth had been here.

A shout from upstairs revealed her clothing, still wet, in the bathroom. The twins hurtled down the stairs, Elizabeth's clothes in hand. "She was here," they chorused in unison.

"I know." Her voice, so rich and commanding began to quaver and her vision swam. Leaning heavily on the wall she realised that she was weakening. "Help me back to the cottage."

Their faces which had begun to show concern at once became business-like and one on either side they helped her back outside.

The storm had not abated and they all began to feel the chill. Anne's mind, totally controlled by Her, was unaffected. Anne's body, however, began to shiver uncontrollably, spasms racking it. It was too much too soon. She could command the body, but not while She was weakened. She needed the fireplace. She needed sacrifice.

*

Geoff pulled himself painfully to his feet. He couldn't stand on his left leg. The waves of pain shooting up when he tried made him nauseous. Hopping to the door jarred his ribs. But he needed to get out. Lowering himself gently back down, he began to crawl. "This is going to take forever," he thought to himself. But he had to keep going. He couldn't be there when Anne and the twins returned. He knew that She had somehow possessed Anne, and the thought terrified him. For some reason She had taken his gift, after all his work for her. After all his life, for Her. His pain-filled senses couldn't let him complete his line of thinking. Why?

He crawled across the clearing to his hiding place, from which he had watched the family every night. It was still dry, overgrown as it was by the large surrounding trees. Curling up he felt along his body. Certainly one rib broken, he thought, and definitely his ankle as well as bruises across his whole body. He knew if he remained where he was he could die, he was wet, cold and naked. He knew the only safe place for him was at his woodcutting shed. But that was nearly a mile from here. In his present condition he was fairly sure he wouldn't make it. But then to stay here was to die. He had to try.

Pulling himself painfully to his hands and knees he crawled through the brush to the path.

*

Elizabeth came through the clearing with a sense of relief. She had recognised the pile of logs from her earlier travels and at least knew where she was now. After walking for so long she had begun to think that perhaps she had taken the wrong path. Which she supposed she had. But whilst she knew that there was a quicker path between the two cottages, she had never used it. The path from here to her cottage, however, she knew well.

The storm seemed finally to be lessening. It had been for the last half hour or so and with it the grey fingers of dawn had appeared. She'd been out all night. Well it would perhaps show the rest of them that she wasn't always going to be there for them. The twins could stop behaving so badly, Mrs. Holman could stop trying to boss her around and her mother, well, she felt guilty about her mother. She was clearly not well.

Feeling slightly chastened, Elizabeth decided to try to get to the bottom of what was wrong with her mother.

As these thoughts and others tumbled through her mind, Elizabeth felt a lot better about herself and began to imagine what her return would be like. They must surely have been worried. Strangely, the thought that she was the cause of this made her feel even happier.

It was then that she saw Geoff.

It was difficult to believe that this wet, mud-spattered creature crawling up the path towards her could be him, but she was in no doubt. She knew instinctively that it was him. He was so covered in mud that it took her a few moments to realise he was naked.

Her previous good humour forgotten, she raced to his side. He was so determined in his crawl that he carried on for another couple of feet before, exhausted, he collapsed.

"Geoff, what's the matter? What's happened?" blurted Elizabeth. "God you're hurt, what's wrong?"

"Help me," Geoff croaked.

"Yes, yes."

"Help me up."

Elizabeth put an arm around his waist and with his arm around her neck, forced him upright.

"I'll take you back to our place," Elizabeth announced, taking control.

"No, we can't. I'll explain later. Just get me to my woodshed."

"What. Why?"

"Listen to me," Geoff grabbed at her, half unsteady, half emphasizing his words. "If we go back there, we are dead. Do you understand? Dead. Help me to the woodshed and I'll explain everything. OK?"

"I don't understand. What's going on? My family, are they OK?" she wailed.

"Look if we don't get out of here now we're in serious trouble. Now come on!"

So saying, Geoff lurched forward and Elizabeth, supporting him, followed. It was only about a hundred yards to the clearing, but it took about a quarter of an hour to get there and throughout the short journey Elizabeth's mind was in torment. It was obvious that something terrible had happened. Geoff was in a state physically and he seemed scared to death of something back at the cottage. Why hadn't he let her go back there for help? With his father to carry him, it wouldn't have taken much longer than it had to limp this little way to his shed. What had happened?

They finally reached the shed and when inside, Geoff directed her to light an oil lamp which hung from the ceiling. Looking down at him, where he lay back on a few dusty old sacks, Elizabeth couldn't believe her eyes. Under the mud he was covered in bruises, his ankle was swollen and looked to be at an unnatural angle.

After lighting the woodburner set in the middle of the shed, Elizabeth set about cleaning him up. A brief spell in the Girl Guides had taught her how to splint a broken bone. But she wouldn't have known where to start if Geoff hadn't taken control.

As she tidied him up and tried to warm him, Geoff began to describe what happened.

Covering her with the coat she lay next to him to try to share her body heat. As he spoke her reaction changed from one of disbelief to outright horror.

This was the 1990s. It might make a good horror story, but this kind of tale was better suited to one of those films which were relegated to midnight on BBC2. Peter Cushing as the wood-cutter and some young woman, her mouth dripping with blood, her breasts forced up into some unnatural position beneath her chin by a tight bodice. No. Things like this didn't happen in this day and age.

Elizabeth hugged Geoff to her and did her best not to laugh out loud. It was true that there had been some strange goings on, but this was something else. Besides if she started laughing she wasn't sure that it wouldn't become hysterical.

To stop him going any further, Elizabeth pulled up his chin and kissed him hard on the mouth. His body had begun to warm and she felt him stir against her. Quickly without thought, she undressed and pulled her to him.

Chapter 9

The red flame began to grow larger as more creatures were brought to feed Her. When She had returned, the flame had almost gone out. She had exhausted herself. She needed to plan, to consider what had happened. But She was so close.

Surveying the living-room, Gods! it was a shambles. The body of the mother lay sprawled, where she had left it, across the settee. It's mind was still functional, but that which was Anne Masterson had retreated before her onslaught into a small recess somewhere. This was not unduly concerning. It was hers for the taking, but somewhere it was finding some strength to resist her, however pathetically. Perhaps it had something to do with the bright white light. Almost as soon as this was considered it was discarded. The woman was disposable, in fact would be disposed of, as soon as She returned. It only had to last until then. But Her poison should have worked, she should belong totally to Her now. The thought nagged at Her despite everything.

The traitorous Holmans sat huddled together by the door. Horror still etching their bruised and lumpen features. They survived now only because She thought She needed them. Come the return, She would rid herself of them as well. They had been gibbering wrecks when She got back earlier and each had screamed their devotion to Her, but they had proved untrustworthy before, who was to say they would not again?

No. She must have total devotion, nothing else would be allowed. Still, at least their wailing had stopped, even if they did interrupt her trail of thought by sobbing every now and then.

As the door opened the Holmans flinched back. The young twins entered leading a young deer. Here was Her future. These children were Hers. It had been their devotion to Her that had finally allowed Her to leave the fire. Their sacrifices which had given Her the strength, if even for a short time. Delicious children, theirs would be the ultimate reward.

Swiftly, the twins killed the deer, it's blood caught in a bowl first, then the heart removed. With these cast upon the fire, She blazed. She could feel Her earlier strength returning. There was no thought now of keeping Her alive. She would be strong enough by evening to again take control. She must. Events had gotten out of hand last night, exhausting Her prematurely now though, She had a plan. The twins looked at one another briefly, nodded and then left the house again.

Summoning the Holmans to Her, they came and pressed their foreheads to the hearth and She gave them their instructions. Impressing upon them the need for their success. This time, no failure would be accepted. This time, failure would result in them dying.

Pleading with Her, they both gabbled out assurances that they wouldn't fail.

Mr. Holman fairly leapt from the room and She felt him leave the house. Mrs. Holman, if anything, was quicker. Gathering the body of Anne Masterson, she put it over her shoulders and gently carried her to the bathroom.

Left alone for a moment, She continued with Her plans. It must be tonight, She smiled inwardly.

It would be tonight.

*

Elizabeth woke stretching, she was momentarily disorientated by her surroundings. Beside her, Geoff turned slightly, but remained fast asleep.

The memories came flooding back. They had slept together. Well, more important was what had happened before they went to sleep together. She squirmed with pleasure. It had been wonderful. No. That wasn't enough, it was better than wonderful. Better than she could have ever imagined and she had imagined this ever since she had met him.

Tingling all over she stood from beneath the coat which had covered them, she gently covered him with it, and again she saw his injuries.

"My God!" she thought, "He's scratched and bruised all over."

His hastily splinted ankle stuck from beneath the coat. It was cold to the touch, but nowhere near as cold as it had been.

Looking to the woodburner, Elizabeth, trying to be as quiet as possible, opened it and added more fuel.

Her stomach rumbled and she tried to think of when she had last eaten. Yesterday? It wasn't clear. She opened the door and looked outside. The sun was already half way down towards the tops of the trees. It was afternoon! She must get home, her mother would be at her wits end. But then if they had been so worried, how come nobody had come to look for her? Surely Mr. Holman knew of this place.

With this came the reminder of Geoff's tale last night. It was ludicrous, but it would explain why they were still here and nobody had bothered them. With doubts plaguing her mind, she dressed again in Geoff's clothes, covering him as best she could, she left the little shed and resolved to go home. Reasoning that she needed some clothes, they both needed food and Geoff could certainly do with some proper medical attention. As loathsome as the idea was, his mother would probably know exactly what to do.

But it wouldn't hurt to be a little bit wary, just in case Geoff's wild story proved to be true.

As she crept out into the afternoon, as careful as she was, she failed to see Mr. Holman rise up from behind the woodpile. Ducking inside the shed he gazed down on his son. Tenderly lifting him, though he hurt all over himself, he carried his boy home. Time enough to sort the girl out later. His first thoughts were for Geoff. Whilst not life-threatening, his injuries had left him in a bit of a bad way and he could do with a bit of cleaning up.

As he carried Geoff back to his cottage, he thought, "She'll never know." Maybe even get the boy to leave when he's better. Sure enough he'd be better away from all of this.

Geoff opened his eyes, looking around and not quite focusing. "Dad, is that you?"

"S'alright lad, we'll get you cleaned up, bit of rest and you'll be as right as ninepence."

"But what about Her? Dad!" Geoff began to struggle against his father's grip.

"Whoa now son," he soothed, "You'll be fine. Let me worry about Her. I'll not let Her have you boy." But how? It was all very well saying such, but practise was a completely different kettle of fish. He knew that if he betrayed Her, he was dead. This couldn't be betrayal enough. She had told him to find the girl. Hadn't said anything about Geoff. Well, he knew roughly where the girl was. Wouldn't take a minute to get her.

Meantime, the least he could do was leave his boy comfortable.

"One thing at a time," he thought to himself, "and first things first." George Holman knew he wasn't the greatest thinker, far from it. But in his own mind, his priority was to his boy, and the devil take Her.

*

Elizabeth felt faintly ridiculous. Firstly, she was wearing Geoff's clothes, the shirt was OK, if slightly baggy. The long sleeves she just turned up. The trousers, however, well, they were gathered up around the waist by a piece of string which looked dangerously like fraying. She had a vague recollection of them falling in a pool around her ankles. So much so, that the further she walked, well, darted from tree to tree, the more she resolved that the first thing she would do was get changed. Then sort Geoff out with some clothes and get him looked at. And only then would she confront her family. With this in mind she stopped at the edge of the clearing to her cottage.

And paused.

In the cold light of day Geoff's story was crazed. But he had all those injuries. Her family had been behaving oddly. She herself had felt strangely attracted to the fireplace.

A small worm of fear had burrowed into her brain. She could feel it there. No matter how stupid she told herself this whole thing was, she couldn't force her feet to move forward. As she stood rooted to the spot, her sisters walked into the house. They were covered in blood, their hands, indeed their arms up to the elbows were covered in gore. Each was cradling something in her arms.

Staying where she was just a little bit longer, suddenly seemed like a reasonable idea. It was still only mid-afternoon, it was quite a warm day, if anything it was still getting warmer. So Geoff should be OK for a while at least. Crouching down to wait, she noticed the chimney, or rather the smoke from the chimney. It was billowing out! On a day like today!

Elizabeth began to consider that maybe, just maybe, Geoff wasn't quite as mad as she had first thought.

After a few minutes the twins left the house and quickly crossed the clearing going directly into the woods across from her. "Give it a minute," Elizabeth thought to herself.

That minute seemed to take an eternity, but she counted up to sixty and stood. She had already decided how to cross the clearing to the cottage. All thoughts of stealth out of the window, she sprinted over to the door, which had been left wide open. Peering around, the hall stretched off. Bright as it was outside, the interior seemed unnaturally gloomy, but the hallway was empty.

Moving quickly but quietly to the foot of the stairs, she heard splashing from the bathroom. Pausing for an instant as curiosity warred with caution, she determined on the latter and began to tiptoe up the stairs, fearful that each step would creak or groan and let someone know she was there.

Elizabeth was just past the halfway point when the bathroom door opened. Mrs. Holman, her sleeves rolled up past the elbow, came out and went into the kitchen. Elizabeth was so shocked, she had frozen. Had Mrs. Holman looked up, she could not fail to have seen her. Whilst she was undecided whether or not that would be a bad thing, Elizabeth had set a course of action and would rather nothing upset it.

However, she couldn't resist leaning over the bannister to see what Mrs. Holman had been doing. "Forewarned is forearmed."

She could not remember where she had heard that, but it seemed that whatever information she could find out could only stand her in good stead. Could only help to make sense of this whole thing.

She was amazed to see her mother laying naked in the bath. Elizabeth shocked herself by nearly calling out, but something struck her as odd. It was her mother, she was asleep.

Without trying to ponder this further, she carried on up the stairs. Just in time as it happened, because as soon as she stepped into her own room, Mrs. Holman started up the stairs.

Again she froze. Looking through the door which she left open a crack, she watched Mrs. Holman cross the landing and go into her mother's room. There was a sound of cupboards and wardrobes opening and closing and then Mrs. Holman reappeared. Without a glance to either side, she started down the stairs.

Elizabeth began to breathe again and was surprised to think that she had actually stopped in the first place. But with her heart in her mouth, she darted across her bedroom and quickly changed into her own clothes. Choosing a warm jumper for herself and an oversize baggy jumper for Geoff. Throwing these and Geoff's own clothes into a holdall, she quietly went back to her bedroom door.

Sneaking a look through the gap she went back to the top of the stairs. A second's hesitation and she opened the linen cupboard grabbing a couple of blankets and stuffing them into her holdall. With a swift mental pat on the back and feeling ever so slightly pleased with her preparations, Elizabeth started down the stairs. A quick look over the bannister revealed the bathroom door shut and assuming that Mrs. Holman had gone back in, Elizabeth quickly descended and peered into the kitchen. Again this was empty. Thanking her good fortune she crossed to the fridge. Grabbing packets of food and stuffing them atop the blankets in her holdall, she pushed a bottle of lemonade into a gap. The holdall was fit to burst. She grabbed the first-aid kit and thrust this under her arm.

As she turned to go, she saw a bottle of whisky next to the cooker and grabbed that as well. Thinking that every eventuality was covered, she slowly edged into the hallway. A glance over her shoulder showed the bathroom door to be shut still.

It had gone like clockwork.

Tiptoeing down the hallway again she was nearly to the door when she felt, rather than heard, someone call her name. It wasn't a call that she recognised, but it was by it's very nature, compelling. Her feet poised to run, turned and she had her hand on the handle to the door of the living-room before she had a chance to think.

"Run!" a voice in her mind called, but it was so far away. Like someone had shouted to her from a great distance. The voice was almost pleading. A man's voice, part of her mind told her.

Torn for a moment between going into the room and fleeing as she wanted to do.

Then the first call came again. Crushing all other thoughts out of the way.

Elizabeth turned the handle and walked into the living-room.

*

Geoff was laying in his own bed. He felt sore in every pore. His father had cleaned him up and re-splinted his ankle. Christ! That had been excrutiating, sending fire all the way to his groin. But it had settled now and his father had given him something for the pain, as well as binding his chest so tight that it was hard to breathe.

He lay thinking of Elizabeth. It had been lovely. He guessed that he had been her first. He knew that she was his. He had always been promised to Her. Since before he could remember he was Hers.

Now She had removed her hand. The very thought made his eyes tear. Whilst in his heart of hearts he knew that what had happened was probably for the best, he felt such a massive sense of loss. Nearly twenty five years since he had been devoted to Her and twelve since he had confirmed that original devotion himself and now nothing. He had never imagined himself without Her. All his dreams, all his desires had revolved around Her. Jealousy engulged him when he thought of Anne Masterson. Bitch!

But then again he thought of Elizabeth. How he, lying there on his woodshed floor, had watched as she had undressed and...

Sighing, he closed his eyes sleepily. The pills his father had given to him were making him drowsy.

His father came back in with a bowl of soup and some bread.

"Try and get something inside you boy, afore you go to sleep," he said gruffly.

It had always been that way with his father, thought Geoff. No nonsense. To the point. But he knew that he loved him.

Placing a hoary palm on his son's head, Mr. Holman pronounced, "No fever. That's good. Your ma would be better for this. I'll see if I can't get her to nip back," but he sounded doubtful. Geoff could see concern and fear in his eyes.

"Don't worry, dad, I'll be OK. But listen, this has all gone too far. She's out of control. She's..."

Mr. Holman's head shot up, half-cocked, on one side, as if listening.

"Stay here boy," he ordered. Then he grabbed his son by the shoulders. "Get away lad. If you ain't up to it now, then soon. But get away." Mr. Holman's eyes began to tear, but he brushed his sleeve over them and then, for the first time since he was a child, his father kissed him. A quick kiss on the forehead and he was gone. Pausing in the doorway only to hiss, "Get away, you hear?"

Geoff tried to get up, but he was too dizzy and fell back.

*

Victoria and Mary stood over the body of a rabbit and looked at one another.

Then came the call.

"RETURN TO ME!"

They ran.

*

Mrs Holman had washed Anne and dried her off. Dressing her had been more than difficult, she was like a huge rag doll. But she had managed. Propping her on the toilet she began to brush her hair.

Suddenly, Anne became animated. Her eyes opened and she looked for a second at Mrs. Holman with a haughty expression. Mrs. Holman quailed, but followed as Anne rose and strode imperiously towards the living-room.

Chapter 10

Elizabeth walked into the living-room. Her mind was so absorbed by compulsion that she initially didn't notice anything else about her surroundings. All at once, the compulsion left her. The vacuum created as it went left her momentarily senseless. Then her own persona filled the void. She staggered both physically and mentally, as her mind reeled from this abuse.

Suddenly sentient, she looked around her. Her mind, still trying to regain control, could not at first ally the present living-room to that which she had expected.

The furniture, the curtains, the television, the carpets, even the wallpaper, was gone. Replaced by a small wooden table, a matching welsh dresser and old rocking-chair. There was a sheepskin rug beside the hearth and of course, dominating the entire room, the fireplace. A dim red light suffused the air. No other light source was discernable. Just the red haze dimly allowing her to see. A fire was lit, but alone it could not be responsible for the light.

"COME TO ME."

The thought virtually exploded in her mind. Her body complied, propelling her towards the fireplace. Elizabeth's mind rebelled against this, to no avail.

She stood at the hearth.

"KNEEL."

She knelt.

"OBSERVE."

She watched as a kaleidoscope of images tumbled in front of her. Through the flames she saw countless lives played out. Everything that had taken place in front of the fireplace.

It began with the twins. Throwing countless small creatures into the flames. Birds, mice, rabbits, some still alive. The deer, killed on this very spot so that it's heart and lifeblood could be consumed by the flame.

The attack on the Holmans made her gasp. How had the twins beaten two grown men and a grown woman? It was impossible. The wolf that had changed into Geoff.

Then it was her in front of the fire, laying peacefully asleep, her throwing the remains of the sparrow on the fire so that her mother wouldn't see it. Thus unwittingly adding to the sacrifice herself.

Mr. and Mrs. Holman, a great deal younger, having sex on the hearth. Sacrifices made before and after. Then a boy child, at first as a babe in arms, but then slowly growing older. Coming by himself to sacrifice to the flame. Performing his own rituals. As the images continued, the boy unmistakably grew into Geoff.

It seemed as though the flow of images was moving back in time. At first it was only the Holmans who tended the fire. Then a whole host of others. Sometimes just one at a time, at others it seemed more than twenty.

Elizabeth thought that she began to understand. The further back in time that the images took her, the greater the numbers. As she was shown more, she began to reason it out. Before her family had arrived the only worshippers had been the Holmans. Two old people and a young man. Mr. and Mrs. Holman could, theoretically, last another twenty years. But what if they didn't? The long line of worshippers could peter out. What the fire needed was new blood. A new generation of worshippers to continue the sacrifices. It was logical enough. A whole new family to join with the old to perpetuate this macabre formula. Everything pointed towards it. Everything that the Holmans had done, was quite obviously working towards this end.

Elizabeth's mind almost crowed in triumph. She knew. Knew exactly what was going on. The only thing now was to try to plan a way out of all this. Extricating her family from the mess that they had gotten themselves into.

Even as this final thought was still in her mind, the images changed. No longer was she shown rituals and worshippers. Now there was just a beautiful young woman kneeling in front of the fire. Behind her the room looked exactly as it had to Elizabeth when she had just entered. The rocking chair, the table, the welsh dresser, even down to the rug that this lady knelt upon.

Time froze for a moment as the lady looked up into the fire, but by chance? She also seemed to be looking directly into Elizabeth's eyes. Elizabeth gazed back at her. God, she was beautiful. Her face was perfection. The most brilliant green eyes, set in a face so pale, the skin without mark or blemish. Her lips so perfect. All framed by a mass of dark hair. The lady's eyes mesmerized her. She could have fallen into those green pools, which looked back knowingly, so assuredly.

The moment was gone. The lady's head dropped back down and from beneath her robe, she pulled out a lump of meat. Elizabeth noticed for the first time that the lady's robe was mud spattered and torn. Her arms covered in blood.

With a cruel smile, the lady threw the meat into the flames.

All hell broke loose. Elizabeth felt herself buffeted by winds. The flames on the fire in front of her chased through a myriad of colours, becoming red. The lady in the image reached into the flame and withdrew the meat and then crammed it into her mouth. Blood and gobbets of flesh oozed down her chin, dripping onto her robe.

For a moment all was quiet, then there were men crowding the room. She could see from the expressions that they were angry, mouths opening and closing soundlessly, fists and arms raised.

The lady raised her arms and for a moment the men crowded back. Then the lady fell, though Elizabeth had not seen what had struck her, fell back into the fire.

The flames in front of Elizabeth blazed briefly and then died. All but the red flame, which came forward dominating the whole grate until a single sheet of flame roared in front of her.

Slowly, in the centre of this flame a figure appeared. Walking towards her, the figure grew larger. As it did so Elizabeth recognised it as the beautiful lady from the final image. She halted before Elizabeth and stood still. That knowing look. The way she held herself. She emanated power. Power and dominian. Elizabeth knelt, completely overawed. At that moment she would have done anything for this woman.

"DO YOU KNOW ME?"

"Yes," replied Elizabeth aloud.

"LET ME ENTER YOU."

"Yes."

"LET ME ENTER YOU."

"Please," Elizabeth tried. "What do I do? I don't know what you want me to do!"

"OPEN YOURSELF TO ME."

"NOW!"

Elizabeth tried. Tried with all her heart. But something prevented her. Refused to let this lady into her mind.

All of a sudden Elizabeth was aware of a brilliant white light pushing back the red. It seemed to come from herself.

The lady's beautiful face was contorted with rage.

"WHO ARE YOU?"

The deep, rich voice of the lady had taken on a shrill quality.

The figure from the white light turned to face Elizabeth. It was her father! "Run!" he shouted to her, "Run!"

Scrambling back on all fours, Elizabeth pushed herself away from the fireplace. Her backwards motion was halted by the settee. The room had returned to it's modern aspect. Using the settee to pull herself up, she stared transfixed as the red light gradually began to overwhelm the white. The figures within facing one another. Her father's white light flared back briefly as he screamed at her to run. But then the red flame was back. Her father's figure seemed to arch in pain as the white light failed completely. Dropping to his hands and knees, Elizabeth heard him call out faintly urging her to flee. But she could not leave him. Tears poured down her face uncontrollably. Laying prostrate, finally his figure disappeared.

Elizabeth screamed.

The lady in the fireplace looked up triumphantly.

"NOW YOU ARE MINE!"

"No," screamed Elizabeth. Standing, she fled to the door.

Behind her she could hear the lady laughing.

She opened the door to a packed hallway. Directly in front of her were her twin sisters. Behind them stood Mr. and Mrs. Holman. Victoria and Mary shared one of their looks and each started forward.

Elizabeth pushed at them roughly, thinking to force her way out, through to the front door and freedom.

"Get out of my way," she shouted. But she might as well have pushed at the walls. They didn't budge an inch. It was impossible. She had thrown them both around before this, both playing and fighting. But now, try as she might, she couldn't move them. Rather, they began to push her back.

Elizabeth lashed out, but the twins didn't even register the blows. Victoria caught one punch, intended for her face, in a tight grip with both hands. Twisting her round until her arm was forced painfully up her back. Mary then grabbed her hair and dragged her over to the fireplace.

"Help me!" Elizabeth screamed at the Holmans. "For God's sake help me!"

Though they looked at one another, neither Mr. nor Mrs. Holman moved. They just stood in the doorway. Mrs. Holman looked on, her arms folded, with a worried expression. Mr. Holman half raised his hand, but then lowered it back to his side. A sad, guilty look upon his face, then he turned his head away. As if he could no longer watch.

The twins forced her to her knees in front of the fireplace and Mary twisted her hair cruelly to make her look into the fire. Tears coursed down her cheeks. Tears of pain, sorrow and anger. All these emotions bursting free and all of them useless.

Elizabeth opened her eyes expecting the lady to be in front of her. But there was no-one there. Just the red flame, blazing up the chimney.

Still held by her sisters, her struggles in vain, Elizabeth sobbed, "Mummy!" over and over again, "Mummy!"

Then her prayers were answered. Out of the corner of one eye she saw Mr. and Mrs. Holman move out of the doorway as her mother entered.

"Oh, thank God you're here," she sobbed.

Mary twisted her sister's head up to look at her mother.

Looking down coldly at her eldest daughter, Anne Masterson replied, "No, thank ME you are here!"

115

But it wasn't her mother's voice.

*

Geoff sat on the edge of his bed, manfully struggling to pull on his jeans. Every movement sent bolts of pain through his chest. Every time the fabric caught on his splints or brushed his ankle, it set his leg afire. Crying aloud with each fresh bout of pain, fighting against successive waves of unconciousness as his brain tried to shut out the agony. After what seemed an eternity he did his jeans up and stood. Although he only put his weight onto his good leg, he knew in his heart that he wouldn't be able to get very far. But he had to try. He nearly passed out again trying to pull on his T-shirt, and again when he pulled on his trainers. But finally he was dressed. Sweat pouring off him, teeth gritted against the pain, he hopped to the landing and gingerly, using the bannisters to support him, he made his way down the stairs.

Casting around he found a broom which, when turned upside down, made a servicable crutch. Feeling as weak as a day old kitten he pushed open the door and hobbled across the clearing. With no clear idea of what he would do when he got there, he headed off in the direction of the cottage.

He had to do something.

*

Elizabeth was stretched out full length on the hearth rug. The Holmans had her arms, whilst her own sister, Victoria, held her legs. Anne and Mary stood above her. Try as she might, Elizabeth could not move a muscle. She had thrashed and torn at them, but it was no use. Pushed firmly down on to the floor, pleading with them, screaming at them. It all fell on deaf ears. Whatever hold She had over Elizabeth's family was total. The Holmans, however, looked too petrified to do anything other than co-operate.

From behind her back, Anne drew forth a knife. Half expecting some sort of ritual dagger, Elizabeth's shock at seeing the weapon increased when she realised it was a carving knife from the kitchen.

Elizabeth screamed herself hoarse, they were going to kill her! It was unbelievable, she was going to die at the hands of her own family! Her own mother! Tears streaming down her face, she screamed "No!" over and over again, imploring the Holmans to aid her. Mr. and Mrs. Holman looked at one another. Mr. Holman gave an almost imperceptible shake of his head, but their shoulders were slumped, as if in defeat.

But Elizabeth was not going to die quietly. Lifting her head from the floor, "Why are you doing this?" she screamed at her mother. "Mum, stop it. Think about what you're doing! You can't kill me, I'm your daughter. Mum!"

"Dear child, I'm not going to kill you, you are to be the vessel of my return. Think of it girl. Your body will live forever, think of the power, the glory. Not death, life eternal."

So saying, her mother turned to Mary, "Are you ready my child?" It was eerie, her mother's face, her mother's beaufitul smile, so proudly looking at one of her children. But the voice was not and never had been hers.

Mary nodded and quickly slipped her sweatshirt over her head, she spread her arms wide. Smiling, she just said, "Now!"

Anne's right hand flashed with the knife and plunged it into Mary's chest. Blood fountained and splashed onto all of them. Anne held her daughter upright by the chin and dug deep into Mary's breast.

Victoria watched, triumphant as her twin's arms slowly fell to her sides and as Anne released her hold, Mary's body slowly fell to the floor, an ugly red hole where her left breast should have been.

Anne's hand was dripping blood as she raised Mary's heart above her head.

Elizabeth's mouth working silently, too shocked to speak, as Anne leaned across her to place the offering into the fire.

In an instant all was quiet in the house. There wasn't a sound from outside.

And then all hell broke loose.

Darkness plunged all around, inside and out the only light was that of the fire which suddenly roared, flames blazing higher and higher. The heat was intense, stones in the fireplace began to crack. The fire irons in the rack leaned drunkenly as they began to melt. Outside the trees were whipped in all directions as winds tore across them. Lightning smashed into the earth from the clouds that hadn't been there a moment before.

Anne's body folded back against the settee, a marionette with the strings cut, as She left her.

Elizabeth, so close to the fire felt her clothes beginning to smoulder, the edge of the hearth rug had already begun to smoke. Even as the heat continued to rise she felt an iciness gather between her eyes. So piercing, like a needle pointed icicle forcing it's way in through her forehead, into her brain.

*

She watched through Anne's eyes as the heart was placed onto the fire. She was stopped in Her tracks momentarily as She felt such a surge of power. It was almost too much. A hair more and it would burn her to a cinder. Fighting for control, she dropped Anne's body

118

and transferred Herself to the fireplace. All around Her She could feel the energies She had created smashing down. It was far greater than She could ever have prepared herself for. With this She could do anything. Exulting in herself, revelling in her power, She could feel herself beginning to lose her grip. Calming herself, she looked at the supine body of Elizabeth. Her chosen receptacle. So young, so beautiful, so fresh. Unsoiled by man. She was perfect.

She began the journey that would bring Her back, harnessing the wild energies that roiled around her, She began her occupation of Elizabeth's body. This would be unlike previously where She had merely controlled their actions. Now She would crush Elizabeth's existance entirely, no vestige of the young woman would be allowed to remain. Clear out the child, to be replaced by Her.

But she was stopped.

What in the name of all her Gods could be powerful enough to prevent her? Certainly not this girl. This child. Gathering herself again, she smashed at the blockage. But it was like a wall. A wall of nothing. Railing against it, she beat herself at it in a fury. It didn't move. Losing concentration she felt her control slipping, the powers were beginning to snap free of her.

"This cannot be!" She raged.

Her spiritual form stood back from the girl's body and looked down at it. She had studied the girl only a while before, only a couple of days ago. It had been perfect. She had made sure of that.

Then it struck her, attempting to replay it in her mindseye, the girl was no longer a virgin!

*

Mr. Holman watched as the body of Anne Masterson fell back, his face, normally so impassive, registered the revulsion he was feeling.

The girl's arm he was holding suddenly stiffened. He looked down at her.

"Christ!" he whispered.

It had been over half a century since he had left Christianity behind and embraced HER, but now as he looked at this young girl he felt wrong. Over the years he had done many things for Her, that were illegal, immoral and down-right disgusting. But at the time they had been the right things for him. He worshipped Her and that was the form of worship She had desired.

But now it was wrong. Whether it was his beating at Her command or whether it was the sight of his son as he had tended him earlier. Something made Mr. Holman turn his back on Her at that moment. Something that completely reversed his opinions and beliefs. Now as he looked down at this poor child, her face a mask of agony and terror, he knew he had to act.

"No more," he stated. Letting go of Elizabeth's arm and standing, "It ends here."

"No, get back!" his wife called to him urgently. Her fear was obvious in every line of her body, "Get back!"

Still holding her sister's legs Victoria hissed viciously, her eyes full of hatred.

"Come on Mrs, let's get this girl out of here."

"No, we mustn't, we daren't."

"I'm not going to let this happen." Mr. Holman's mind was made up. Adamant, he would not be shifted.

Victoria hissed at them again, "Grab hold of her arms. Now!"

George Holman looked at her a trifle warily. Who knows what the little cow is capable of? But even that did not deter him.

"George, no!"

He made to pick up Elizabeth's body from the floor and that was the last thing he ever did.

A jet of pure red flame lanced from the fire and engulfed him completely. In a second he was a human torch. His face, hair and clothes burned away in an instant. The pain was excrutiating, so sudden that he never knew what had hit him. Falling backwards, he landed on the settee which also caught light.

Mrs. Holman leapt up to help him, but Victoria was quicker. She knew something must have gone wrong, but was powerless to help her Mistress. However, she knew that the treacherous Holmans had finally shown their true colours and acting instinctively, she struck Mrs. Holman a powerful back-handed slap. Mrs. Holman, unbalanced, fell into the fire. The heat was so intense that she caught fire before she had landed. Trying desperately to catch her fall, Mrs. Holman put her hands out, but as they hit the hearth her hands stuck. A moment was all it took. Face down in the fire, she was dead almost before the pain registered. Almost.

*

She gazed out at the devastated room.

The traitorous Holmans had perished by the flame, as was right, but unforseen, they had also set fire to the room. The furniture was well ablaze.

Anne Masterson's body lay where she had left it. Her remaining faithful acolyte was staring nonplussed at the fireplace which was now beginning to crack apart.

Finally, she looked down at Elizabeth. Her carefully laid plans had all gone awry. Again. This could not be. This will not be.

The vast ocean of power bequeathed to her earlier had all but dried up. But there was still enough if she acted quickly, acted now.

*

It was into this scene from hell that Geoff Holman eventually staggered. Exhausted, he was overcome as soon as he entered the living-room.

Flames were now licking the ceiling, and thick black smoke roiled out across the woods.

His clothes were soaked by the downpour that had caught him as he hobbled from his parent's house. The deluge that coincided with the mother of all lightning storms, centred on this cottage. He knew before he had seen the finger of red flame leap into the sky above, shooting a hundred feet from the chimney. He knew that he was going to be too late. But with a supreme effort, at the last of his strength, he made it.

Elizabeth.

His only thought was of her. Through the smoke he could dimly make out other figures, but his eyes landed upon Elizabeth as she struggled to sit up. He had to get her out.

As he made his way to her side, she looked up and her eyes met his. She looked dead inside as if she'd been given such abuse that she'd never smile or laugh again. Recoiling for a second from that haggard, haunted look, he had to know.

"Are you OK?" he asked. What he meant was, are you still Elizabeth? But he couldn't bring himself to ask her.

She nodded dumbly.

Stretching out his free hand he helped her to her feet. He had to hurry. They surely only had seconds left.

"My mum," Elizabeth cried.

"She's gone," Geoff hoped it sounded reassuring.

"No."

"Come on, we've got to leave. Now!" Geoff tried to drag her, but he couldn't.

Elizabeth pulled her arm free and knelt by her mother. She was breathing.

"She's alive, help me. Come on."

Geoff tried to help Elizabeth to carry Anne outside, but his damaged body wouldn't allow him. Feebly pushing from behind he followed Elizabeth as she dragged her mother outside.

They got as far into the clearing as they could before Elizabeth dropped her mother onto the ground.

The cottage was now well alight. Flames were roaring from every window. The noise punctuated every now and then by a crash from inside.

"My parents..." began Geoff.

"I'm sorry," Elizabeth cut him off. She bent over Anne's body.

"But..."

"Look, they're dead, alright?" Elizabeth couldn't drum up any sympathy for them. Bastards had all helped to kill her.

Anne's eyes opened.

"Liz," she croaked.

"It's OK mum, you're OK."

"Where are the twins? What's going on?"

Anne tried to sit up, but her strength failed her. "Where's the twins?" she demanded.

"Mary's... mum, Mary's dead."

"No," Anne put her hand to her mouth, "No," the shock hadn't hit. But Elizabeth grabbed hold of her mother and pulled her close.

"Vicky, where's Vicky?"

"She's, uh... she's still inside."

Anne got to her feet slowly, "Vicky!" she screamed, "Vicky!"

Elizabeth held her back and looked imploringly at Geoff.

Geoff nodded to her, understanding immediately.

"I'll go."

So saying, he turned back and hurried to the cottage. Taking a deep breath and holding his arm across his face, he limped across the threshold and disappeared from sight.

Anne and Elizabeth waited. It seemed a lifetime. Crashes and explosions boomed out across the clearing, deafening them. They huddled together, hanging on to one another, helpless. Anne's sobs shook her body, the knowledge of Mary's death pushed to one side by the hope of Victoria's salvation.

Mourn the dead, but care for the living.

A great groaning rose above all the other sounds, followed by a tremendous ripping crash as the roof caved in.

Both Anne and Elizabeth screamed in unison.

But at that moment a small figure was hurled from the living-room window to lay on the ground.

Elizabeth dashed forward and snatched Victoria's body away from the fire's hungry flames. Carrying her back to her mother, she noticed that Victoria was remarkably unscathed. It was a miracle.

Victoria was still breathing, and while her clothing was slightly singed, she appeared to have come out of it without a scratch.

Elizabeth helped her mother to her feet and together they stumbled away from the cottage.

Behind them the cottage had burned to the ground. As she had known, Geoff hadn't made it out.

EPILOGUE

The morning after the fire, Anne was beginning to regain control of her emotions and with this, control of events. She gathered her two remaining children and took them back to the clearing. The cottage was gone. In it's place was a charred ruin. Still smoking. Little glimpses of red still showed through the rubble. Testimony to the ferocity of the fire.

Across from them was the car.

Anne was desperate to get away and hurried them into the car. Thankfully it started first time.

She had thought long and hard all night. She had no recollection of anything since they had arrived here. She knew deep down that she had to notify the authorities, but tell them what? She didn't know anything. Elizabeth had refused to talk, distancing herself from her mother, and Anne hadn't felt able to talk to her last night. Not with Mary gone.

But today she knew she must.

She had to get to the bottom of this.

"Elizabeth," she started, "Listen love, we'll get away from here first, but you must tell me what's happened. We'll get through this together, but I must know."

Elizabeth nodded, tears forming.

As they began to drive through the woods Anne continued, "We'll go to the Police, they'll have to be..."

She was interrupted by Victoria who reached forward, placing a hand upon her shoulder. With a slight shake of her head, Victoria said, "No, mother, actually we won't."

As her mother nodded her agreement, Elizabeth screamed.

It wasn't Victoria's voice.